DARK WATERS

LUCAS PEDERSON

SEVERED PRESS
HOBART TASMANIA

DARK WATERS

WWW.SEVEREDPRESS.COM

ISBN: 978-1-925711-92-9

USS CUTTER-Captain Emily Duncan's final transmission to Admiral Wade - 6:00 am, August 3rd. Received August 6th:

"Admiral Wade, we have been bumped off course, though by no fault of our own. Per my last transmissions, we are low on fuel and still waiting on the tanker. But I fear with the thing in the water bumping us farther and farther off course the tanker will miss us. I have sent you our last known coordinates via Ping. Though I know we're doomed. It's toying with us now. The breach in the hull cannot be patched. We are taking on too much water. Our only hopes are the escape pods. That's if we get to them in time…"

PART 1
DEAD GODS, LIVING MONSTERS

CHAPTER 1

Sharks! Always the sharks. They swarm in like vultures of the sea, snatching dead fish out of clients' hands before darting out of sight. And, oh how the people gasp and cheer. How they laugh through the mics in their diving masks. They are so mystified by these gliding beasts, they forget what lurks in the murky waters just beyond their sightline.

They always forget.

The sharks feeding from their hands are small blues. Vicious, but with the right protective gear, they're fairly harmless. And that's the fairytale aspect of a dive. You're so well protected from the smaller sharks, you forget the ocean is a very big, very dark place.

They always forget.

And that's why Miles is here. Because, they always forget. While the clients are whooping and awing over the majestic beauty they're submerged in, he watches. He waits. In the screen of his helmet are three smaller screens, all showing him the perimeter. His drones drift and scan, relaying the images in real time. Even his eyes have eyes.

It's what he's paid to do. To keep these tourists safe while they forget the terrors circling. While they forget they are being hunted constantly.

This day, however, appears quite calm. Nothing more than a sea turtle with six eyes drifts by Drone 2. A couple small tuna dart by Drone 1. Drone 3 drifts without incident. Works for Miles, though. Gives him a moment to ready himself more. They are about ten minutes into the dive. Nothing deep. About thirty feet or so. In a clean section off the broken California coastline. The state is little more than a sliver after the big quake of 2030. Then came all the melting glaciers and rising seas.

All this before the Great Climate Change happened. Which really fucked everything – and everyone – up. The world, quite literally, turned itself upside down and inside out and…well…in a sense anyway.

Oil is a depleting thing, not that Miles cares much about the stuff. It's his belief oil is a form of evil and drives that evil into the hearts of men. So many wars have been fought over fucking oil, of all things.

It's the water that concerns him. Aquafers are drying up and as far as he knows there's only three or four major ones still bountiful. In America, at least. Why the hell none of those smartass scientists haven't figured out a way to filter ocean water or something, is beyond Miles. It's as though the bastards enjoy watching people suffer.

Of course, it doesn't help that most of the country is owned by MJ Oil, either. Those bastards are the epicenter of oil. It's their first concern. The owner, Murdock Jones, even ran for president one time. Miles thanks whatever god there is the pompous asshole didn't make it to the end. And—

Something blasts by Drone 2, shaking it. When the image clears, all that remains are silvery bubbles.

Set twenty yards away from the group, the drones are his first line of defense, and his extra eyes.

Miles' heart quickens. *Here we go.*

His grip tightens on the AR 300. A special assault rifle designed for underwater combat. Dual clips. One is loaded with deterrent slugs made of nonlethal hard rubber. The other is the real deal. With a press of a button, he can determine a creature's fate.

He has only used the real rounds on two occasions. Both fully warranted.

His finger hovers over both buttons now, waiting to see if there is a true threat, or a rogue dolphin toying with the drones.

All drones reveal murky waters, and little else.

He waits. While the tourists laugh and *ooo* over the wonders of the deep, Miles watches, and waits. He moves away from the group a bit. The group's guide, Emma, shoots him a concerned look as she hands one of the people a dead mackerel. He waves a dismissive hand at her. Could be nothing. But, as life has shoved in his face again and again, it's better to be prepared than not at all. Or even a little. One must always be fully prepared for anything. And that's not just the Navy Seal in him thinking. He has learned that being prepared is the key to everything in this horrendous life.

He watches. He waits.

Almost ten minutes pass and he checks his air supply. Still have a good seventy percent left. Which the tourists have as well.

When he glances at the drone screens, Drone 3 is all large teeth and a gaping maw. The screen goes black.

Shit. He swivels in the direction of Drone 1, knowing full well what owns those large, dagger-like teeth. He presses the fatal button on his rifle and lifts it, ready.

And yet, it does not attack.

Miles glances around, slowly. The murk hides things. It's a predator's greatest tool. Still, the thing doesn't attack. He checks Drone 1 and 2. Nothing but more murk. Another clear sign that shit has gone bad, however, is the lack of fish and other aquatic life. All there is…is silty salt water and seaweed.

The small blue sharks, obviously realizing shit just got real, dart away from the group.

There's a lot of aww's, and sad faces, and slow detachment from the fairytale water world. But it's for their own good, really. They need to wake up now.

Sent via direct link, Emma says, "Should I lead them to the surface?"

Using the direct link, so the clients don't hear, Miles says, "Not yet." He scans the area. "Hold tight. Try to get them in a tighter group."

"What's out there this time?"

"Could be a White. But…I don't know." He ventures farther away from the group. "Just keep them close to each other. Promise them more blues, or something. I don't want a straggler getting snagged."

"Will do."

She's a good woman, Emma. Smart, strong, funny. Although he'll probably never hear the end of it from her when they surface. She is his voice of reason. When they are out of the water, anyway. Below the surface, he needs to be in command. She's the guide. He's the eyes with the gun. Although, she can kick any shark's ass…there are other things out there. With all the quakes and melting ice caps…things have been released. Mutations have occurred. The oceans are far more dangerous than anything in the world. Especially with all the unknown creatures swimming through them nowadays.

Like the leviathan beast Miles read about a few months ago. Some incident on an old oil rig. Barely a paragraph in the news. Something about an Iowa oil driller named Braden or Bracken who was the sole survivor in an attack by a sea monster he simply called a leviathan. There were no details, really. Just that he survived, and the monster had tentacles. That it killed his entire team.

Then there's the shit he saw before retiring from the Seals. Things nightmares are made of…

These waters now, however, have fallen still. The murk is like a wall even his remaining drones can't see through. He needs new drones, though. Ones that track movements would be nice. As it is, however, he's stuck with what he has, and they haven't failed him yet.

Yet...

"Anything?" Emma sounds a bit irritated. Which is okay. Better irritated than someone dead.

"Shh," he says.

In his ear, she sighs.

Miles turns slowly, gaze floating over the not so distant murky water with its bits of seaweed and kelp and silt. He glances toward the surface, finding nothing gliding above them.

He releases a heavy breath, opens his mouth to tell Emma all is well, when something bashes into his back with enough force to drive him a few feet from the clustered group.

"Oh my God, *Miles*."

He flips, head over flippers, for a moment, then rights himself, trying to ignore the pain spreading through his upper back. At least his tank wasn't compromised. At least—

"*Miles!*"

He's half-turned when he sees it. A gaping mouth with rows of long, fang-like teeth. Miles kicks, diving low and somehow manages not to get his legs chomped off. He swivels, sand kicking up and making visibility nearly impossible for a few godless seconds. When the sand clears, the creature is gone. Or rather, out of sight. The terrified group of tourists are holding each other and even though Miles can't hear them, he's sure they're spouting off some kind of prayer or weeping. More than a few have probably pissed themselves.

Emma floats near the quivering group, gaping at him. She says nothing, but then again, she doesn't have to. Her wide eyes behind the clear mask are enough.

They also tell him what he already knows.

It's not a shark.

He rights himself, bubbles wobble in front of him. He checks his drones, though neither show signs of life. Whatever is out there, it knew to avoid the two drones. Snuck in where Drone 3 would have covered.

Heart crashing against his ribs, Miles swivels, rifle up and ready.

Silence, only obliterated in fragments by his own breathing and rumble of bubbles from his exhale, surrounds him. His sight drifts over the group, shoots beyond them, flicks to the drone screens, and he turns, back to the group. If the thing attacks again, he doubts it will go by the drones still active. It knows Miles can see it, somehow, through the drones. So, it will avoid the things.

Or eat them, like it did the other one. If it does that, he'll be blind out there in the murk.

Flashes of the past snap at him like vipers. Memories of being in the deep darkness of the warm Atlantic. Of his team being picked off one by one by some unseen, untraceable creature. A creature he killed, though just barely. The very creature that aided in his decision for retirement.

At thirty-nine, he is the youngest to retire from the Navy Seals. Despite the offers to return, he has gladly never looked back.

Even so, the memories still haunt him. And, perhaps, they'll haunt him forever.

Shaking his head, he refocuses himself to the here and now. He hasn't lost one tourist yet, that's what makes him so sought after. He's the best at what he does.

Sucking up his fear, he blows out a long breath. His nerves ease and he falls into a thin battle fog. Where everything appears sharper, clearer. The murk doesn't hinder him. No. Indeed, his focus is like a search beam in the dark. Happens to all soldiers from time to time. Some, more often than not. For him, it happens even during everyday happenings. Like buying groceries. It's both a curse and a blessing, he supposes. Still irritating as shit when it happens on the outside and in society, though. The looks he gets…

Focus sharp, Miles scans the area. But as time rolls away, nothing more happens. Nothing shows itself.

His oxygen tank is at forty percent. Okay, but not ideal. He'll give it another—

It blasts out of the murk like nothing he has ever seen before. The tail of a shark, fast and true, but the head is a misshapen version of a Great White. The teeth are far too long, too pointy, but the facial structure is nearly the same.

Then there are the arms…and hands…

Arms like a human stretching out, long hands grasping. All covered in gray skin.

Never has he seen such a monstrosity.

He lifts the rifle and squeezes the trigger. The creature jerks and twitches, blood swirls in the water. Miles kicks away from the monster's surge. Its snapping jaws snag onto one of his flippers, yanking back as its massive head thrashes back and forth. One of the long-fingered hands grips onto his leg, dragging toward the sharp maw. Miles bends, slams the muzzle of the AR 300 to the creature's head, and puts roughly twenty bullets into its brain. Blood tendrils out of dark holes and the hand releases his leg. The jaws relax. He yanks himself away from the thing as it rolls, belly up and bobs in the water.

Miles closes his eyes, allows himself a few careful breaths and says to Emma, "Get them to the boat. Fun's over."

Emma doesn't argue and leads the group to the surface.

Miles stares at the dead creature still bobbing in front of him, trails of scarlet spilling out of the many holes in its head.

A mutant. Some sort of human/shark hybrid.

He's not sure if it's human pollution that creates such monsters, or spores thawing from the melting ice caps. And really, what does it matter? The beasts are here. They are roaming the waters. There's no rhyme or reason. They just...are.

Miles shoves the dead creature away from him, signals for his drones and heads for the surface.

CHAPTER 2

The entire ride inland, Emma is staring at him with a strange glare he can't quite figure out. Something between awe and horror. Maybe a little bit of anger mixed in there somewhere. He can't really tell and all he can do is shrug. Not knowing what someone else is thinking is the worst. Even if he can somewhat figure out what's on her mind, he's never sure until the clients leave.

Once they are in the office, though…

Miles shoves the thought out of his mind for now and plasters on a fake smile for the guests. Best not to alarm them any more than they are. And really, they've already pretty much forgotten what happened back there. Oh, they'll go on and on about the little blue sharks feeding from their hands, but the monstrosity that might have killed them…? No. That's too scary to share. Too scary to even think about. It proves science is right and whatever they believe in is skewed. Can't have that. No, no, no.

He turns away from them to look out over the shimmering water behind the charter. The sky is a mix of gold, pastel pinks and purples. Dusk swallowing up the day. The waters reflect these colors, mingling green-blue in with everything creating a gorgeous, glittering stew. How something so beautiful could hold so many horrors has always perplexed Miles. Sunsets are one of the draws of tourists, ah, if they only knew the monsters swimming just under the surface.

Maybe they're the lucky ones, though. Not knowing what stalks the oceans *must* be a blessing of some sort, right?

Oh well, he'll listen to Emma yell at him a while when they dock, then go have a few beers with Mike. Little brother is due to port around eight tonight. Been far too long since Miles has hung out with Mike. Then again, Mike is a busy man in the Navy these days. At least he didn't get into the Seals, like Miles. The Seals do more swimming. And swimming leads to meeting your worse fears eye to eye and praying you live to tell the tale.

Working on a battleship, though…perfectly safe. Well, from the creatures below anyway. It's other humans one must worry about on a big ship. Torpedoes and shit.

The Pacific isn't like the Atlantic, Miles muses as the charter speeds toward the docks. The Atlantic is choppier. Always at some kind of unrest. Even the southern half, it's like the waters just can't sit still these days. Ever since the climate shifts, things are all messed up. North is warm and tropical. South is colder and bleak. Antarctica is little more than a medium sized island, though rich with all kinds of recourses rich men clamor over each other for. Not many succeed however, because the Atlantic has become a violent body of giant waves. Even a huge cutter ship will capsize. Yes, the Atlantic is a stormy, mad bastard.

The Pacific, though, it's almost serene. Like a vast sheet of glass stretching on and on into forever without end. The farther south one travels, the waters get a bit unsavory, but nothing at all like old Atlantic. The middle Pacific, although the deepest of all the oceans and harboring the worst of creatures – as far as his experience goes anyway – is no doubt the quietest. Maybe that's why the monsters dwell in the fathoms here. It's big and deep and calm.

"Docking," Emma shouts and Miles snaps out of his thoughts.

He moves to port, as Emma slides the charter along their large stretch of dock. He hooks a rope over one of the poles, carefully pulls the charter closer to the dock, ties the rope tight to the loop on the boat. He does the same for the bow. Once the charter is secured, he helps the clients out of the boat and on to the dock. Laughing and patting each other's backs, the tourists make their way toward the beach.

Before Miles can gather the diving gear to bring back to the office for recharging, Emma pushes him. Nothing hard. It barely made him step back. But enough to get his attention. Her face is something close to hellfire. Hot, red, eyes like brimstone.

"What the *hell* was that?"

Miles shrugs, continues picking up the gear. "Mutation, I reckon."

"Not the monster," Emma says, voice full of growls. "You. Where were you down there? You're supposed to communicate with me. That was the deal. That's why I hired you. To communicate any dangers and help protect the clients."

He snorts. "And load and unload the gear. And recharge the tanks. And—"

"Don't be an ass." Emma takes a few slow breaths, nods. "Okay, so you do more than I hire you for, but damnit, today you dropped the ball out there."

"I killed it, didn't I?" Miles tosses some diving gear onto the dock, goes to gather some more. Seagulls cry out all around him. Most annoying fucking things he's ever encountered, seagulls.

"You did. But, Jesus, Miles…it was a close one."

He grunts, finishes tossing the rest of the gear onto the dock and turns to her.

Emma is about three years younger than him, deeply bronzed skin and dark hair. She's gorgeous, and if he didn't have any morals, he'd ask her out for a beer or something. Maybe even begin a relationship. Ah, but those damn morals keep getting in the way, don't they? Every time he thinks he might ask her, he chokes the words down and says something dumb.

Like now. "Lost one of my drones out there. Need a new one before we go back out."

She sighs. "I'll get one on order."

"Good. Maybe order two. Four might be better." He manages a faint smile. "Don't worry, I'm not flaking out on you."

A slight line forms between her green eyes. Something he finds absolutely adorable. She shakes her head. "I don't think that at all, but maybe you were a little distracted today? When does your brother get back?"

He snorts. "I wasn't thinking about him. I know he's fine."

"Then what were you thinking about out there, other than protecting the clients?"

He looks away. "Nothing, really."

"You're a piss-poor liar, you know that?"

Miles shrugs, turns and hops onto the dock, offering her his hand. "Doesn't matter what I was thinking about. The day is done. C'mon, Boss."

Emma rolls her eyes but takes his hand and he helps her onto the dock. For a moment they are so close their lips nearly touch. Miles feels the very heat of them and yearns for a taste. But he backs away before he makes that mistake. He's been down the relationship rabbit hole more than once, and each one ended badly.

He smiles, steps back and says, "I'll get the cart."

Before she can say anything, he hurries down the dock to retrieve the motorized cart made for hauling the gear. Best not to delve too deeply into anything. Besides, she has never showed him anything that proves she feels the same way. He'd be a fool to even try, really.

He hops into the cart, drives to where Emma stands by the gear on the dock, and loads up. Then, with her riding shotgun, he drives them to the office, leaving those seagull bastards in the dust.

At the office, which is little more than a large shed, Miles replaces a couple of oxygen tanks and recharges the rest.

There was a time when he'd probably have to send the tanks elsewhere to be recharged, but these days Emma made sure they were up on the latest tech. Well, next to the latest anyway.

He still wants his motion-tracking drones, but...heh, what can he do? He's not the boss.

Once all the gear is charging and put away, he walks down the short hall to the main office...and stops a few feet from the door. A frown creases his face. There are two other voices coming from Emma's office. Both male, judging by the deepness of them. And both seem to have the same monotone of Government officials. He can't make out what they're saying, but for as much as they're talking it must be of some importance. Then, all at once, they stop talking.

The door opens and Emma rushes out. She spots him standing there, skids to a halt and places a hand over her chest. "Jesus, Miles. Don't sneak up like that!"

"I..." Miles glances at the open doorway. "What's going on?"

Emma sighs, shakes her head and says, "I was just coming to get you. They're here for you."

Miles doesn't move, staring at the doorway. "Who's here for me?"

"Just get in the office. It's important."

Miles' hand falls to the butt of the pistol on his hip. One can never be too wary around the Government these days. But he follows Emma into the office nonetheless.

Emma's office always has an odd hint of vanilla and he could never figure out if she has some kind of air-freshener or it's her perfume. And as usual, the office is warm. Almost to the point of being uncomfortable.

Seated in front of Emma's messy desk are two men dressed in identical blue jeans and black sweaters. One was black like Miles, the other a big blond dude with icy blue eyes Miles didn't like at all.

He nods at the men, hand still resting on the butt of his pistol.

"Miles Raine?" The black official asks.

Miles nods again.

Both men stand and face him.

Here we go, Miles thinks and flicks the holding strap off his pistol.

But the men don't reach for weapons. Instead, the blond one steps forward, face very solemn. "We want to extend our greatest sympathies, Mr. Raine."

Miles frowns. "What? What the hell are you talking about?" He glances at Emma, but her head is lowered. She's crying. Tears drip from the tip of her nose to the desk.

The black official sighs, pats the blond guy's broad shoulder and says, "You are the brother of Michael Raine, correct?"

Miles glances from him to the blond man, and back again. "What the fuck is going on?"

"I'm Agent Rogers," the black man says. "And we're here to tell you that the battleship, USS Cutter has been destroyed. No survivors have been found." His eyes shift away from Miles and he sighs once more.

"I—wait, what? You're telling me Mike is—"

"We don't know for sure, but it is likely," the blond man says.

Heart crashing against the walls of his chest, Miles staggers away from them. He shakes his head, eyes swimming in tears. "No. No, he was supposed to come back tonight. We were going to have a couple beers."

"I am so sorry, Mr. Raine," Rogers says.

"You have my condolences," the blond man says.

"So, it's like that, huh?" Miles shoots a glare at both of them. "You're gonna just assume he's dead?"

"The damage," the blond man says, "was quite extensive. Whatever was left of the USS Cutter is now at the bottom of the North Pacific."

Miles blinks. "H-how'd it happen? Sub attack?"

Both men glance at each other. Then Rogers says, "We're not one hundred percent certain yet."

"The hell does that even mean?"

"I'm Agent Dent, by the way," the blond man says. "And it means we're still investigating the situation."

Miles angrily swipes tears from his cheeks. "Well, Agent *Dent*, that doesn't help one fucking bit, does it?"

Dent nods and steps back a bit.

Rogers says, "Admiral Wade requests your presence, Mr. Raine."

Miles snorts, still wiping away tears. "Well, you can go tell him to fuck off."

Rogers steps closer, face firm. "It is not a request."

"I really don't give a shit what it is," Miles says. "I'm out of the military. Been out for three years now."

"That doesn't matter to Admiral Wade," Rogers says. "But we may have reason to believe your brother and a few others might still be alive."

Miles looks from Rogers to Dent and back again. "What?"

"Come with us," Dent says, "and Admiral Wade will fill you in."

"We're not at liberty to divulge such sensitive information."

"Mike might still be alive?"

Only Rogers nods the slightest bit. Barely.

From her desk, Emma says, "I need a vacation anyway. Go see what this Admiral Wade wants, Miles."

He blinks at her, sighs, and returns his attention to the agents. "Alright. Let's go."

CHAPTER 3

No one speaks the entire ride to Fort Everdeen, the nearest Naval base not far from the coast. The one, Miles knows, where Admiral Wade rules.

He'd met Wade a couple of times. Once during a briefing while Miles was still a Seal, the other when Miles retired. Both times, Admiral Wade gave Miles a slight chill.

The man just has a cold look about him, practically seethes ice. From the cool, blue eyes to the expressionless, pale face. Admiral Wade is the greatest for a reason. And Miles feels it's because the man simply has no compassion. That, and he's highly intelligent.

Before Miles' final mission with the Seals, Wade somehow predicted the enemy's movement. And despite the advisors' recommendations, he changed the mission into one of seek and destroy, instead of a covert seize and rescue. According to Admiral Wade, the enemy would be located on a small island near what used to be Hawaii. They would be concentrated on the north side of the island, ready to retaliate with heavy artillery and sub-nuclear bombs. The advisors said it would be wise to come in from the south, and while the enemy was distracted, Miles and his team, Dagger Point, would sneak in, grab the intel and bugout before the bastards even knew they were there.

Wade, however, he challenged the advisors' plan, claiming it was foolhardy and weak. No, they would enter from the western side of the island, come in hot and mow the enemy down, which was estimated to be about sixty men. Dagger Point, God knows, has taken out more than that before. Wade's mission was to go in, take out the enemy, retrieve the intel and return home. He claimed if they came in from the south, the enemy would be watching.

Lo and behold, he was right. When Miles and the Dagger Points landed on the western side of the island, as they snuck close to the encampment, they noted sentries monitoring the south.

Remembering this now, as the car passes by the gate of Fort Everdeen, Miles smiles. Wade might be a cold bastard, but he's also a smart one.

The car parks in front of the Admiral's Office and Miles gets out. He waits for Agents Jones and Dent and they lead him to the doors. The heat of the day is noxious and he just thanks whatever gods are up there that he's not in the dryer regions where the sand is like grains of toxic waste. Sharp, it will cut the skin and infect you. Plus…there's some nasty creatures out there. Some kind of hybrids the military had been working on at one time and abandoned, then all the radiation resulted in further mutations.

Dent places his wrist against a black plate set into the doors. A small beep sounds, and the doors swoosh open. Dent steps aside and gestures for Miles to step inside. He does, though not caring for the two agents trailing him. He likes people he doesn't trust within sight. Still, he figures they don't want to harm him, otherwise they would have already.

"Second door on the right," Jones says behind him.

Miles sighs, stops at the second door on the right, and glances at the agents. Both nod for him to go in. He opens the door and steps into Admiral Wade's office.

He expected to find the old Admiral seated behind a massive oak desk, leering at him with those cool blue eyes. Instead, the office is crammed full of people and Admiral Wade is staring out his only window, hands clasped behind him.

Miles quickly deduces who the extra people in the office are. Four scientists, a Master Chief standing tall and blank and leaning against the wall on the right, and two more people he can't place. Definitely not military, judging by their civilian clothes and wide wandering eyes. *God*, Miles thinks, *they look like tourists.*

Before he can even announce his presence, Admiral Wade says, "Master Chief Raines. We've been waiting for you."

"Just Miles," he says. "I'm retired, remember?"

The other Master Chief grunts, as though Miles said something slightly funny.

Miles shoots him a glare, rolls his eyes and fixes his attention on Wade, as the older man turns to face him.

"You're never fully retired from the Navy, son." A grin flickers over Wade's heavily lined face. "Just dormant."

Miles nods. "Whatever, Admiral. I'm here because there might be a chance my brother, Michael Raines, might still be alive."

"You're addressing a superior officer, Master Chief," the other Master Chief booms.

Miles slips the idiot another glare. "I suggest you get your ears cleaned. I'm retired. And I really don't care what the Admiral says about it. I am done with the Navy and trying to live my life."

Admiral Wade chuckles. "Son, let's not get into a pissing contest. Master Chief Bennet is on our side and will be assisting you. So, I suggest you two learn to get along."

Those cool blue eyes rest on Miles and it takes all his strength not to look away.

Finally, Wade claps his hands together sharply and says, "Okay. Thank you all for coming. You each had your own private briefing, well, except for Raines." He points at the four scientists. "Play the audio for Master Chief Raines."

Miles frowns. "Audio?"

"From Captain Duncan of the USS Cutter," one of the scientists says. A small woman wearing thick glasses, dark hair tied into a tight bun. She taps on her tablet a moment and holds it up. "A compilation of logs leading to the Captain's final entry."

For a moment, there's only static, then…

"Captain's Log – July 19th. No one is sure, not even myself, why we keep getting bumped off course. And we are indeed getting bumped. We all feel it and hear it every time it happens. If this continues, I will bring it up to Admiral Wade."

Wade says, "I never received anything from Captain Duncan."

"Captain's Log – July 22nd. Our fuel reserves are depleting. I put a call in for a tanker. Whatever keeps bumping us, the extra fuel needed to veer back on course is creating a problem. I just hope the tanker can get to us before we're entirely out of fuel. I have sent a distress call to the Coast Guard and Admiral Wade."

Static. Miles glances at Wade, but the old man only shakes his head and sighs. Not quite meeting Miles' gaze.

"Captain's Log – July 26th. First Mate Raine has spotted something very large under the water while out looking for signs of the tanker. He said a part of it surfaced. Its back, he thinks. But it appears to be circling the ship. We were once more bumped off course, but I fear returning to our original course now will deplete our fuel too much so I am redirecting course. I sent Admiral Wade our new coordinates along with the Coast Guard. I have heard nothing back from either one as of this entry."

Miles blinks at Admiral Wade. "How did you get these logs?"

The old man waves a hand. "All of it came through to me at once. Even the distress calls. Tried contacting Captain Duncan multiple times with no response. Our drones have picked out a large oil slick near her last known coordinates, however."

"Captain's Log – July 30th. It bumped us harder this time. The hull has been breached and we're taking on water. I have sent out multiple distress calls with no response. We're alone out here. Why aren't my calls going through? The crew is trying to patch the breach as best they can but reports from my engineers is…pretty grim. If the breach cannot be patched up, I will have to deploy the escape pods and abandon ship."

The scientist lowers the tablet a bit and says, "We did receive a failure to launch ping from USS Cutter's pod bay."

Miles frowns. "So, the pods weren't deployed?"

"We believe that a couple of them were. But something got in the way of the others."

An icy chill stutters his heart. "Like what?"

She shakes her head. "We have no idea." She lifts the tablet up once more.

"Captain's Log – August 2nd. The crew is getting restless. They want to fight back at whatever is toying with us. First Mate Raine suggests trying our new anti-sub cannon to eliminate the creature. An idea I need to consider…"

"Captain's Log – August 3rd. I am getting us off this ship. The pods travel faster and we might be able to outrun whatever is trying to sink us. The hull is filling up too quickly to wait for rescue."

She places the tablet on Wade's desk. "This was Captain Duncan's final entry. We received these, along with her distress calls and transmission directly to the Admiral, yesterday. Our drones did capture something about six miles from the oil slick where we believe the USS Cutter sank." She gestures to the blank wall where Master Chief Bennet leans. He blinks and steps aside as the woman scientist taps something, a small device, in her hand.

On the wall, an image of the open Pacific Ocean sweeps below a flying drone. Then the motion slows while the drone's camera zooms in and focuses on something very large slithering in the water, just under the surface.

Miles steps closer to the wall and the dark, slithering image. His eyes widen. "What…what the hell is that?"

Someone behind him, maybe one of the scientists, clears their throat. "We're not certain, but we think it might be—"

"Jörmungandr," a heavily accented voice spouts.

The entire office falls silent around Miles. He turns to find a hunched, older woman with thick silvery hair in tight curls and a heavily wrinkled face staring at him with eyes even cooler and bluer than Admiral Wade's. She shuffles in front of the four scientists.

Those icy eyes never leave Miles. "Midgard Serpent, to those who don't know."

He places her accent as Scandinavian, or there abouts. Far north. A place of snow and ice and cold. It's the only continent left unchanged, as far as Miles knows. And Midgard. He knows that word from somewhere.

"Thank you, Geri," Wade says and places a hand on the old woman's narrow shoulder. She shoots a venomous glare at the man. "Miles, this is Geri Rask. Renowned Scandinavian historian and archeologist. She was the one who found what's believed to be Thor's hammer, uh—"

"Mjölnir," Geri grumbles and adds, "Idiot."

Wade grunts, pats Geri's shoulder and moves away from her. Her eyes find Miles once more.

"Thought no one could lift Thor's hammer?" Master Chief Bennet says from across the room.

"Mjölnir," Geri corrects, hard blue eyes shifting away from Miles. "All the gods have fallen. The weapon lost its power the moment Thor fell. Perhaps you should open a book sometime, eh?"

Miles snorts. Oh, he likes her.

"How do you know for sure that's Thor's hammer?" Bennet steps beside Miles and Miles moves away from the man. "Could be just some old blacksmith's hammer for all we know."

Geri's gaze darts to Wade. "Can I stab him?"

Wade chuckles. "No. No you may not." He addresses everyone. "Boys and girls, since we don't know exactly what we're dealing with here, Ms. Rask has been asked to assist in the finer details of mythology." He glances at Geri and sighs. "I mean ancient history. This serpent might be responsible for USS Cutter's demise and I want you all to be prepared for—"

A sharp knock on the door cuts the words from Admiral Wade's mouth. He stares at the door, a single white eyebrow lifting. "We are in a briefing."

The door opens, and a man dressed in perhaps the brightest white suit Miles has ever seen strides in.

"I'm just in time then."

The man's black hair slicks back from his tanned forehead, held by gel...or something slimy by the look. He brings with him the strange mongrelized odors of oil, vanilla, and cinnamon. A scent that makes Miles gag a little. His thick, black mustache lifts as he smiles. His green eyes sparkle in the soft light of Wade's office. He barely gives Miles a glance on his way to Admiral Wade.

"Admiral Wade," the man announces, extending a hand. "How are you?"

Wade does not shake the offered hand and gives the man a withering glare. "Mr. Jones. Murdock. You can't just come bursting into my office like this, as I'm sure you know. If you'd like to make an appointment, then maybe—"

"Oh," Murdock says waving a flawless, manicured hand. "No, no, no. No appointments. I'm here as an aid to your mission."

Wade blinks. "And how do you know about the mission?"

With a snort, Murdock pats the Admiral on his shoulder. "Come now, you and I both know I know everything that's going on in this country."

Miles' hands clench into tight fists at his sides. Murdock Jones. The oil overlord of America. The man that is said to have aided in the second Civil War all over race and oil. The man who supposedly owned the old oil rig where that Bracken guy lost his entire team to a leviathan. The tycoon who has practically ruined America single handedly.

"That doesn't give you the right to barge into my office like this," Admiral Wade booms. "I don't care who you are and what your connections are. Get out of my office until you make a goddamn appointment like everyone else."

With his back to Miles, he can't see Murdock's expression, but he figures it's somewhere between shock and disdain. One of the most powerful men in America isn't used to being talked to like this and Miles has gained a new respect for Admiral Wade for doing so. He never thought the old bastard could be so awesome. And that's a stretch, really…

"Well, Admiral," Murdock says and steps away from Wade. He observes the others in the room, this time his gaze lingers on Miles a bit longer before moving on. "I help fund For Everdeen, as you know. And I have come to provide more funds for this mission. All state of the art equipment. Mechs, if you wish."

Miles shakes his head. "No mechs. I read about how they failed against the leviathan a couple years ago."

Once more, Murdock's intense gaze finds him. "Ah, but that's where you're wrong! If not for the mechs there would be no survivors."

"There was only one," Miles says, leveling his sight on Murdock. "And even he said he was lucky in the article I read."

Murdock waves a dismissive hand. "All drama, that one. What if I told you there were three survivors and Bracken was just looking for a way to make money because he was poor?"

"Bullshit," Miles says and turns to Admiral Wade. "I want my old team." He hooks a thumb at Murdock. "And I want nothing to do with this asshole."

Admiral Wade nods. "Done. Report back here at twenty-one hundred."

Miles shoots Wade a salute, spins and hurries out of the office before he kills the human stain known as Murdock Jones.

He's just stepping out the doors when a white cloud bursts in front of his face and he knows no more.

CHAPTER 4

Emma is locking up the office around nine at night when a vehicle pulls up near the dock.

She frowns, but keeps to the shadows near the office, kind of happy she hadn't gotten the outside lightbulb replaced. She presses herself into the deeper shadows, watching.

From out of nowhere, a black inflatable boat drifts onto the beach near the dock. A man dressed in all black hurries across the small boat, jumps onto the sand, and pulls it onto the beach a bit. Then he glances in Emma's direction. For a few godless seconds, she feels like she's totally exposed and he can see her. Soon he'll sprint over the beach and slit her throat from ear to ear and…

But he soon looks away and focuses on the vehicle parked in front of him.

A moment later, two other men drag what looks like a body from the backseat. They haul it, one holding the arms while the other hefts the legs, toward the inflatable black boat.

Just above the vehicle is a tall lamp and Emma soon realizes who the men are carrying…

"Miles," she whispers and claps her hands to her mouth, hoping the men didn't hear her.

Apparently they don't because they never stop and load Miles into the boat. The two who loaded him run back to the vehicle, get in and drive away. The man in the black inflatable boat, pushes off the beach, gets in and starts what she assumes is a trolling motor by how quiet it is. Then it backs away into the darkness of the ocean.

Heart galloping in her chest, Emma emerges from the shadows and runs to the beach.

Very faint, she hears the whir of the small motor.

She almost gets into the charter to follow, then dismisses the idea. The charter is loud. It's a brutish beast. The man in the boat would hear her the moment she started it up.

"Shit," she says, staring into the dark void in front of her. There is no moon. No stars. It's like looking into a black wall.

Miles went with the agents earlier. Could this be part of that?

No...this is something different. The military don't knock you out and load you into a boat at night. Or do they? Maybe they do now? No. Something else is going on...something bad. And...

Her sight snags on a fourteen-foot aluminum fishing boat resting on the beach she hasn't had the heart to get rid of yet. The boat had been her grandpa's. The motor is long dead, but it has oars, by God.

Without letting her brain get in the way too much, Emma shoves the boat into the water, places the oar-pins in the holders, and rows away from the dock.

She's about thirty yards out before she realizes she has no clue what direction the man in the boat took Miles. And it's too dark. Too—

Something thumps against the bottom of the boat. Small waves lap along the sides making hollow thunking sounds. Emma sucks in a sharp breath, as if slapped across the face. The boat rocks for a moment, then stills.

Okay, so maybe she should have let her brain get in the way a bit more because there are bad things out in the ocean, especially at night. She glances around, but the dark waters reveal nothing. And it's so damn quiet.

Emma turns the boat around and begins rowing toward shore.

God, I'm an idiot. She rows the boat, pushing herself to work faster. Sweat streams down her face. *Calm down. Freaking out isn't gonna help you. Just breathe, lady. Besides, it was probably just a dolphin.*

The bow of the boat shoots upward in a spray of water. Emma screams, and when the bow crashes back down, spraying her with more salty water, she stares straight ahead.

"*So* not a dolphin."

Not wasting time, she continues rowing. She can make out the parking lamp. The beach isn't far now. Maybe twenty, or even fifteen yards. Water splashes onto her from the right, drenching her in liquid cold. *How can the warmest part of the ocean be so fucking cold?* She doesn't know and right now it's just her mind babbling on in its panic. As if often does.

A whine gathers in her throat as she rows. Her arms are on fire, burning and aching. Her lungs sting from all the heavy breaths in salty air. Sea water drips from the tip of her nose. Her heart bashes itself against her ribs.

She rows.

Why the hell had she not stopped to think about going after Miles? About not knowing which direction the inflatable black boat went and the darkness of this night?

She rows.

How far away from the beach is she? Fifteen yards? Ten? So close. So—

A shiny, black claw slaps onto the side of the boat, inches from her left oar, stopping her progress. She can only see the claw from the lamp in the parking lot. A weak light, but just enough. The boat tilts to the left, right side lifting out of the water. Emma scrambles, back slamming to the right side. She grabs the oar out of the holder and brings it down as hard as she can onto the claw.

There's a giant spray of water, but the claw releases the boat. It slaps back onto the water.

Trying to control her breathing, and failing, Emma slips the oar back into the holder and rows. She doesn't stop until sand grits against the metal bottom of the boat. A shrill squeal sounds behind her and she fumbles over the boat to the bow. She jumps out of the boat onto the beach, landing hard on her side in the sand.

Before she has time to crawl away, the boat is yanked back into the water and soon pulled under.

"Jesus," she mutters and hauls ass away from the water, not stopping until she reaches the parking lot where she collapses in a dripping, wheezing heap.

Low chuffing noises find her ears. She snaps her head up, eyes widening as she stares down onto the beach into a set of large, glimmering eyes like silver coins. It's about ten feet from her, stopping in mid-crawl. Its black skin shines under the dull light of the lamp, much like the long extinct orca. Its long, black claws dig deep into the sand. She can't make out what the head looks like, nor if it has legs or a tail and fin. None of that matters.

Emma gains her feet, standing on wobbly legs, and the thing on the beach surges forward, moving much like an angry crocodile. And it's here she sees it does indeed have a tail. One very much similar to a shark. She stumbles backward, but the creature stops just short of the lamp's full glow. It hisses, revealing rows of long, shimmering teeth, shoots a glare at Emma, then scuttles backward through the sand and into the water.

A series of shivers runs through Emma.

She makes it back to the door of her office before her legs give out. She struggles with her keys, unlocks the door, crawls inside and kicks the door shut.

Wheezing, heart still slamming, she manages to crawl a few feet from the door before collapsing again.

This time, darkness crowds in and before long…she's swept up in the dark waves of unconsciousness.

CHAPTER 5

Voices in the darkness draw him out of sleep.

At first, they're nothing but mumblings, though soon he manages to pick out words here and there.

"...can't..."

"...he'll be pissed..."

"...we should step back."

"Is he awake?"

"...dunno..."

"He's awake."

Miles' eyelids flutter, letting in tiny glimpses of pale light. He swallows, hating the dry click in his throat.

"Miles?"

He doesn't answer and instead turns onto his side. His mouth and throat are like strips of old carpet. Dry...dusty.

There's a constant acrid stench in his nostrils he can't get away from. His head throbs and by all accounts, he feels like he's waking up during the worst hangovers in the history of hangovers. His stomach gurgles and a sour belch grumbles out his mouth. Every time he tries to fully open his eyes, the pain in his head slashes like hideous claws.

"Miles?" Same voice as before, and like before, he ignores it.

For now, all he cares about is not feeling like hammered shit on a fiery anvil. He needs water. Something cold and wet. Anything. Anything to wash the dry coating on his tongue and throat away.

Before he can even ask, someone says, "Here. Just a sip, though."

The brim of a cup is pressed against his eager lips and slowly lifted. Cool water spills over his cracked lips and into his mouth. He swallows. The water ignites a thirst in him that cannot be denied. He latches onto the offered cup, yanking it out of the person's hand and upending it and gulping the rest of the water down.

"You get sick it's your own fault, man."

That voice. He knows it from somewhere. The same smartass tilt in tone.

But every time he tries to open his eyes, they burn. So, he forces them shut. "Where am I?"

A snort and then hot, moist breath puffs into his sweaty face. "First rule of a Dagger...ask questions later."

Miles opens his mouth, shuts it and tries to open his eyes again. The sting is too much. "Alright, asshole, why do my eyes burn?"

"Pretty fucking demanding for being a prisoner, aren't ya?"

He can't stop the chuckle bubbling up his throat. Once this subsides, he shakes his head. "I'm not a prisoner."

"Oh, you're not? Weird. Because I think it's you in the chair and—"

"Jakob," Miles says. "Shut the fuck up and tell me what's in my eyes."

The other man sighs. "You're still a cranky ass, even after all these years."

"All these – it's been three."

"Like I said, all these years."

"For shit sake, Jakob," a deeper voice said. "Wash his eyes out."

Miles knows that voice too. "Hey, Guether."

"Master Chief."

Icy water splashes into his face.

A grunt. Then, "Hold on Master Chief. I gotta get inside the eyes."

"Just hurry it up, will ya?" He almost forgot how annoying Jakob is. Almost.

"Yeah, yeah, yeah. I'm trying. Ya gotta work with me here, man."

Miles forces his eyelids open as far as he can (no more than slits), and another massive splash of ice water hits his face, this time more than a little gets into his eyes. It burns for a moment, but at least he's able to open his eyes some. His vision is blurry, like looking through an opaque window. Yet one more splash of icy water strikes him full in the face. Then another. And another. And—

Miles bursts out of the chair, sputtering. "Jesus, you trying to drown me?"

Jakob laughs, though no one else says anything.

Gradually, Miles' vision clears enough to see. Leaning against an old wooden table, large and expressionless, is Guether. He crosses his large arms over his broad chest. His bald head gleams under the lights and his long, blond beard still reminded Miles of some Viking warrior from forever ago. In front of him, Jakob cocks a dark eyebrow. His face is still very boyish, youthful. His vision isn't fully restored yet.

"Others are resting up," Guether says.

Miles nods, goes to rub his eyes.

"Uh," Jakob says. "Don't do that. I need to keep washing your eyes out until you can see clearly."

Miles lowers his hand. "The fuck is in my eyes?"

Jakob glances away. "It was Milan's idea."

"It was all of our idea," Guether booms. "Don't be a damn wuss. Remember our little talk about owning up?"

Jakob waves a hand at the big man. "Yeah, yeah. Okay, so it was a collective thing. But still, I was kinda against it."

"You were the first to agree."

"Well, not intentionally."

"Bullshi—"

"Okay," Miles says, feeling the onset of a damn migraine. "What the hell is going on?"

"It was Admiral Wade's idea," Jakob spouts.

"More our idea," Guether says.

"Whatever. Point is, we got you away from there."

Miles sighs. "Keep washing my eyes out."

It takes Jakob another four splashes with ice water before Miles can see just as well as he had before they shot the white powder (whatever it is) into his face.

Vision crystal clear, he glances from Jakob to Guether and back again. "I think you two better tell me what's going on here."

"Wade rounded us up yesterday," Jakob says.

"More like a group call," Guether says.

Jakob shoots a frown at the big man. "You tellin' this story, or am I? Jesus jumpin' on lily pads. Some people…"

"Listen," Miles says. "I don't care who tells it, I just want to know what's happening."

"Master Chief," Guether says.

"Not anymore. Stop calling me that."

The big man pauses, sighs. "Okay, Miles…Admiral Wade contacted us yesterday and said you'd need us. He set-up a plan to make it look like you've been abducted."

Miles blinks. "Okay? Why?"

"He said he has a feeling Murdock Jones might make an appearance and he didn't want that pompous prick to own you," Jakob says.

"So, this was all planned?"

Both men nod.

"Lovely. And what the hell did you guys spray in my eyes?"

Jakob gives him a crooked smile. "Mixture of chloroform and Sills Crystal."

"Sills—those crystals are forbidden!"

Jakob titters, appearing utterly insane. "It is! Ah, but it worked out just fine."

"For you, maybe," Miles says. "That about killed me."

"Hardly," Jakob says. "The Sill was minimal. I personally saw to that."

There are no windows in what Miles assumes is a basement of some kind. The walls are made of ragged, sweaty stones. The bare light bulbs dangle on red and black wires from the ceiling. There's also a strong smell. Something earthy and sour. Dank is the word he's looking for. The floor is old, black dirt. Oiled dirt, he assumes by the other, fainter odor.

"So," Miles says. "This was all planned, huh?"

"Yup," Jakob says. "He also gave us all the gear we need. This is top-notch shit, man."

Miles looks from Jakob to Guether. "You all know I'm going after my brother, then? That I don't give a shit about the Cutter otherwise?"

"Our mission," Guether says, straightening, "is to find any and all survivors and eliminate any and all threats."

"Is that so?" Miles smirks. "I say we do what we need to while out there."

"You don't feel a bit sorry about all those who died?" Jakob frowns at him. "Shit, you're colder than I remember, man."

Miles nods. "My personal mission is to find my brother, Mike. But if we find more survivors, we'll help them."

Guether reaches over and punches Jakob in the arm. "Told ya he still remembers how to kick ass."

"Ow, dude," Jakob says, rubbing his arm and glowering at Guether. "Okay, okay. Stop hitting me, asshole."

Guether shakes his head. "You're such a little wuss, for a Seal."

"I'm the fucking medic, man. Calm your tits."

"Listen you little—"

"My God," Miles says. "You two haven't changed a bit."

Jakob winks. "We like consistency."

"You're an idiot." Though Guether is smiling.

"So," Miles says. "What's the plan?"

"Dagger Point goes in and saves the day, like usual, man," Jakob says.

Miles shakes his head. "It's not going to be that easy. We'll be in open water with something huge."

"The Admiral has a few things that might help us with that," Guether says.

Jakob chuckles. "Yeah, like a fucking tank, man. Probably even better."

Gaze drifting between the two men, Miles sighs. "Maybe you guys should let me in on what the hell is going on?"

Guether straightens, smiles his crooked smile. "Eat first. Admiral says we have to shove off in a couple of hours."

"Right." Miles glances around. "So, um, where are we?"

Jakob pats his arm and gestures for him to follow. Guether falls in behind Miles as they walk to a set of rickety, old wooden stairs leading up to a closed door.

"Safe house," Jakob says, clomping up the steps. "Wade sent us this location. Everything is fully stocked too. Pantry even has goddamn gummy bears, man."

"You're an idiot," Guether grumbles behind Miles.

"You're just jealous I won't share my gummy bears."

Guether gave a heavy, "*Humph.*"

The steps creak and groan under all three men's weight. Jakob opens the door and bright light stabs into Miles' sensitive eyes.

As they gather into a kitchen, Miles says, "Do me a favor. Next time just send me a text or something, okay?"

Laughing, Jakob snatches up an open bag of gummy bears. "Man, we couldn't. Wade thought your phone, everything, might be tapped. The only way to get you away from For Everdeen and here was to fake your kidnapping." He pops a few gummy bears into his mouth and chews.

Miles shoots a glance at the stainless-steel refrigerator, then his sight drifts over the kitchen. Compared to the ugly basement, this room is amazing. Clean and shiny. Everything appears new or at least relatively so.

"So, who is Wade so afraid of?" Miles takes the bag of gummy bears from Jakob and stuffs a few into his mouth, realizing how long it has been since he's eaten anything.

"Murdock Jones," Guether says and opens the fridge.

God, Miles hates that name. "But why is he so afraid? Murdock can't stop him from sending us out."

Rummaging through the fridge, Guether says, "It's not that. And the Admiral isn't really afraid. More like he doesn't trust that pompous asshole."

"Yeah," Jakob says. "After what happened to that dude in the South Pacific and Murdock's connection to it…Wade knows the douchenozzle might double-cross him."

"The leviathan, you mean?" Miles frowns. "What was his name? The guy that survived…"

"Boaken," Guether spouts.

Jakob snorts. "And you call *me* the idiot. His name is Bracken, you damn mongoloid."

Miles rolls his eyes and hands the gummy bears back to Jakob. The younger man nearly jumps with joy. "I need real food. What do we have?"

"Eggs?" Guether asks.

"Sure. Would rather have a steak, though."

"Why not both?"

Miles blinks. "You *have* both?"

Guether chuckles, rummages through the fridge a bit and brings out a carton of eggs. He places them on the small table, returns to the fridge and when he turns back to the table he plops a thick package wrapped in white butcher's paper next to the eggs.

The big man grins. "We have both, my old friend."

"Ah, shit," Jakob says. "Here comes the bromance."

"Shut your face," Guether says, stabbing Jakob with a glare.

Jakob waggles the bag of gummy bears in front of him. "Sweet sugary goodness."

The big man rolls his eyes and looks at Miles. "Sorry, Sir, but you'll have to cook it yourself. Moron and I need to catch at least an hour nap before we head out."

"Mmmm," Jakob says, making a show of eating the gummy bears. "So chewy and sweet and fruity!"

Guether sighs and points toward the archway across the room. "Bedtime, jackass."

Jakob nods. "Okay, okay. Yeesh, dude." He places the bag of gummy bears on the table and follows the big man out of the room.

And just like that, Miles is alone.

He quickly finds a saucepan for the eggs and a broiler pan for the steak. He sets the oven to broil and has never craved a cigarette as much as he does now. Quitting a year ago had been the best decision, but even so…he still craves a smoke from time to time. He enjoyed smoking. The taste, the calm which follows, everything. Cigarettes also helped him think deeper than without. At least he thinks so, anyway.

Miles turns the burner for the saucepan on to medium heat and plops a nice thick cut of steak onto the broiler pan. He seasons it with salt and pepper and a sprinkle of garlic salt. A few minutes later, the oven beeps to tell him the correct temperature is achieved.

He places the steak in the oven and waits until the meat is nearly cooked before slapping a few tablespoons of butter into the saucepan and cracking open a couple of eggs. He dashes each with salt and pepper and checks the steak, stomach grumbling.

It's still a bit bloody, but not bad at all. He pulls the steak out of the oven and slips it onto a plate. Once the eggs (sunny-side up) are ready, he scoops them onto the steak. In the silverware drawer he finds a steak knife and fork.

He's shoveling the steak and eggs into his mouth a moment later at the table.

He tries not to think about anything, but that's impossible. Murdock wants him for something, but what? The man in white barely gave Miles any attention in Admiral Wade's office. What the hell does the bastard have to gain through all of this? There's no oil involved, after all. So, what the hell would benefit him being involved in a search and rescue mission? Makes no damn sense.

He's chewing the last piece of steak when—

"Whoa, slow down tiger."

Miles looks up, finding his formally second in command, Jenna Thomson, smiling at him, arms folded across her chest.

He swallows and says, "How long you been standing there?"

She chuckles, heading for the coffee pot. "Long enough to know you're kind of a pig."

He watches her place a pod into the top of the coffee machine and set a mug under the spout. She touches the BREW button and it begins gurgling. Then she faces him. He has forgotten how beautiful she is. Though feminine, she's all muscle. Her oval face, green eyes, and olive colored skin...he could never really stop looking at her.

Like now, he finds it difficult to look away.

"You're lucky the guys still like you," she says.

"Why wouldn't they?"

She grunts. "You kind of abandoned us, you know."

Miles sighs. He knew this would come up eventually. Had actually lain awake some nights thinking about it. And even in the silent, dead of night, he had no real answers besides...

"Sorry. I needed to get out."

"You left without even saying goodbye. Totally ghosted us."

Another sigh blows out of him. "Sorry."

Jenna waves a dismissive hand and turns to the full cup of coffee. "Oh, no worries. I know that last mission got to you pretty bad. So do the guys."

A shiver slithers through him at the thought. He tries to shove the memory back into the depths of his mind, but, the more he tries, the more it forces itself in front of his mind's eye.

All those teeth...and the little girl...

Miles finally manages to shake the memory back, realizing Jenna is staring at him. He shrugs, not really sure what to say.

She frowns, sips her coffee and sits in the chair across the table from him. "It still bothers you, doesn't it?"

He chuckles humorlessly. "I wouldn't say bother." He glances away. "More like haunts."

"Have you ever talked about it to anyone?"

His sight snaps back to her. "And tell them what? That I let a little girl I could have saved die?"

"You couldn't save her, hun," Jenna says, eyes softening. "None of us could."

He stands, grabs his plate, "I could have," then he puts the plate in the sink. "I had time. I could have stopped it."

When he looks, Jenna blinks at him. "You saved so many kids that day. Just think of how many would have died if you followed orders."

"But I didn't save them all. The look in her eyes…" He shakes his head, sighs. "Never mind. Tweedle-Dee and Tweedle-Dum mentioned something about a tank made for water?"

Jenna, visibly giving up on him, shrugs. "Pretty much." She eyes him. "How do you know about this…thing?"

In the fridge is a single can of Pepsi. He plucks it out and shuts the door. Then cracks the can open. It's been so long since he had soda of any kind and he gulps half the can down, belches and shrugs. "Some Old Norse creature, according to the lady historian, what's her name. Gebbie? Gessie? G—"

"Geri, idiot boy," the old woman shuffles into the kitchen, snatches the mug of coffee from Jenna, takes a swig and hands the mug back.

Jenna, eyes wide, glances from the old woman to Miles. "What just happened?"

"Looks like she drank some of your beloved coffee," Miles say, grinning.

"Name's Geri Rask." She moves closer to him, ice-blue eyes narrowing. "He said you were a smart one, *ha*!"

Miles smiles, despite himself. The woman has some fire in her, that's for sure.

"So, you're the expert Admiral Wade sent us?" Jenna frowns. "I thought you'd be…taller."

Geri whisks a bunched, liver-spotted hand in the air. "Pah! I have taken apart tougher girls than you, dear."

Miles chuckles, he can't help it. The look on Jenna's face is something in the gray area of bewildered and angry.

Finally, Jenna rolls her eyes. "So, you're the expert. What are we up against?"

Geri cackles. Something so witch-like, a sheath of lumps forms over the skin of Miles' arms. She shuffles toward Jenna and points at her. "A *god*, girl. That is what you are up against. And no underwater tank is going to stop it. Jörmungandr has lived a long, long time."

Jenna nods slowly. "Like the Wendigo."

Geri snaps her fingers. "*Exactly*. Only older, girl. Much older. Older than even the Old Norse. As old as the seas…"

Miles clears his throat. "Well, that's great and all, but how do we kill it?"

Shooting him a dark look over her shoulder, she says, "There is only one way to kill Jörmungandr, and it is not with bullets."

"Then...what?"

From one of the deep pockets of her crimson cloak, she brings out a foot long, curved tooth. She holds it up in front of him. "Fenrir. His venom is the only thing to kill her."

"What the shit is Fenrir?" Jenna reaches out to touch the tooth and Geri yanks it away.

"Fenrir was Jörmungandr's brother, foolish girl." Geri backs away so that she faces both Miles and Jenna. "Both offspring of Loki. But this does not matter. What matters is what is in this tooth." She holds it up. "Only Fenrir could defeat his sister. Only Jörmungandr could defeat her brother." Her cool, blue eyes stare at the tooth. Her wrinkled mouth twists downward, as though overcome with some deep sadness. "She won the last time they battled thousands of years ago now."

Miles holds up his hands in a surrendering gesture. "Hold on. You're saying these gods, or whatever were real?"

Geri hisses at him. Actually hisses. "Jörmungandr is real, is she not? You saw her." She waggles the tooth at him. "Does this look like an ordinary wolf's fang? The gods, all of them, were once very real. Most of them have fallen and perished. But a few still remain here. Some are still...angry."

"Angry about what?" Jenna asks.

"Of what man has done to their fallen. How they have all been forgotten and labeled myths. They once ruled over us, you know. We worshiped them, and they were magnificent."

"If they were so magnificent," Miles spouts, "then how come they fell?"

Tucking the long, curved tooth into her cloak pocket, she fixes a glare on him. "When people stop believing in gods, gods fall. They die. They vanish. Most of them, anyhow. Others are too fueled by rage they refuse to die until they destroy the very species that ended their brethren. Men."

Miles nods. He doesn't totally get it but understands enough to let the subject drop. He's never believed in a god anyway. Not so much to worship one, anyway. After all the shit he's been through, he's pretty sure no gods exist. And maybe Geri has a point there too. Maybe so many people stopped believing in a god, all gods, even the almighty Christian one, have fallen. He doesn't know, and there's not time to dwell much on it anyway.

"Okay," he says. "So, we stab that tooth into it and it just dies?"

There's something in the old woman's sidelong glance that unnerves him a bit. Disdain? Malice? Bewilderment? Shit, he can't pinpoint it.

"What you do, Mr. Raine," she says and creeps toward him. He stands his ground. Barely. "You take Fenrir's fang and put it in her eye. Sink it deep to let the venom in. That's how you kill Jörmungandr." She looks away. "That's if we see her, of course."

"You think it – she, won't be around?" Jenna asks, looking a bit too hopeful.

Shaking her head, gray hairs flailing, she says, "No telling if she will or will not be. Best to be prepared."

Miles points at the bulge in Geri's cloak pocket. "How would we even get close enough to put that in her eye? Just curious."

Her cold, blue eyes measure him, up and down. "You are the big man in charge here. You tell me. Harpoon would be too slow and wasted effort, I would think."

He nods. A harpoon, though? Shit, is this the Captain Ahab years? No, it'd have to be attached to something so fast not even an alleged god can dodge it. This is the most crucial thing they need to nail down before they set out.

"A torpedo?" Jenna ventures.

But Miles shakes his head. "Not fast enough. Might as well be shooting a harpoon."

Jenna flaps her arms in exasperation. "Well, shit, I dunno, then."

An idea pops into his head. "Is Ma here?"

Jenna frowns. "Yeah. But she doesn't—"

"She knows every laser-fire weapon known to man," Miles says, easily falling into his old roll of command.

"A laser would burn that tooth up, though," Jenna says.

Miles smiles. "Not if there's a stopper."

She shakes her head, a line forming between her green eyes. "Stoppers never work."

He looks at Geri. "If that tooth is from a god, can a laser destroy it?"

Geri appears a bit perplexed for a moment. She glances away, sucking on her teeth. She shakes her head. "I do not know. Fenrir had already fallen at the time of his death. He was mortal. So, his fang is somewhere between godly and of this world. Know this, however, when I found Fenrir in the catacombs of your very own America, his body had not rotted. Thousands of years and he seemed to only be sleeping. A huge beast in a tight cave, I managed to pry the fang from his upper jaw. As far as lasers though...I just don't know Mr. Raine."

Miles, very gently, pats her shoulder. "Thank you."

Geri blows out a breath, not quite a sigh. Mostly to herself she mutters, "I should have told the Admiral to go fuck himself."

Smiling, Miles finishes his soda and tosses the can in the trash. He looks at Jenna. "Show me this...tank."

CHAPTER 6

Consciousness returns to her in a gray, lazy tide. Slow…quiet.

No.

Not quiet. There *is* a sound.

Like a dog scratching at the door to be let in. Nails raking along wood.

Emma rolls onto her side. She's in the narrow entryway leading to the short hall between her office and the shop where Miles spent most of his time. She coughs, realizing how dry her throat is. Her head throbs and when her fingers touch a spot on her forehead a sharp pain bites into her skull. She tries looking at her fingers to see if there's any blood, but it's too dark here.

And where the hell is that scratching coming from?

She manages to sit, head pounding, vision swimming, and nearly falls over. If not for the wall, she just might have. Instead, she places a hand on the wall to keep her upright until her vision clears and the slamming in her head eases to dull throbs.

Slow, almost methodical, the scratching doesn't stop, and it takes her only another moment to realize it's coming from the door in front of her.

A breath snags in her throat like a fishhook. Her heart bashes her ribs. She kicks herself away from the door. Shaking her head, tears filling her eyes, she knows exactly what is scratching at her door.

The thing from the beach. The thing that almost tipped her boat over.

As if in confirmation, a low growl rumbles, muffled through the door.

That's when she realizes…the door isn't locked.

The thing from the beach has hand-like claws. All it will have to do is reach up and turn the knob and it'd get her.

Suddenly, her bladder feels too heavy. Her stomach…too sour. Her throat clenches and hot saliva fills her mouth faster than she can swallow it down. Before she has time to do anything, she whips to the side and vomits onto the tiled floor.

Wiping her mouth with the back of her hand, she scrambles for the door and turns the deadbolt lock. It finds its home with a satisfying click.

This done, she scoots away from the door once more. The scratching pauses briefly, then grows frantic. A shrill squeal leaks through the door.

She doesn't know what it is. Maybe even Miles wouldn't know. But she figures it's another mutation. Has to be, actually. There's no other explanation of the creature scratching on her door.

After a few minutes, it's obvious the thing can't get through and Emma gains her feet. She leans against the wall, letting vertigo do its thing. Once the world rights itself, she turns and makes her way to the office. The sounds of the scratching follow her.

Once in the office, she shuts the door and locks it, then collapses into her chair. She stares at the black screen of her computer monitor for a long time, before an idea creeps up in her mind.

She turns the computer on and goes to the stored surveillance footage. She's not exactly sure how long she's been out, but maybe an hour or so. So, she taps the footage from about two hours ago.

For the first hour, there's nothing. Then, at the one hour-twenty mark, the black vehicle she saw earlier pulls up to the parking lot lamp. Two men, one big and burly looking, the other shorter and skinny, haul Miles out of the backseat of the vehicle. Here, she pauses the video and zooms in, trying to catch anything she can use to figure out Miles' possible location.

The larger man is bald with what appears to be either a white or blond beard. He's dressed head to toe in black. No patches or anything signifying military involvement. Mercenaries, then?

The smaller man, with his darker skin and thin build reveals much of the same. All black clothing, nothing more.

Whoever these guys are, they know what they're doing.

She zooms out a bit and touches PLAY. A scene she has already seen rolls out. The two men carry Miles to a black, inflatable boat where another man waits. Here, the lighting is worse, but Emma pauses the video again and zooms in.

The third man, it's hard to tell much of anything except…

"It's a woman," Emma whispers to the empty office. The more she zooms in, the more it becomes fact. The person in the boat is a tall, well built woman and she nearly single-handedly hauls Miles – not a small man – into the boat.

"Jesus," she mutters, zooming in some more.

She's about to close the video when something catches her eye. Not with the woman, but the boat. A single word printed on the side, barely readable.

A smile spreads along her face. "Bingo."

The word is: SOUTHBOUND

Emma turns off the computer and hurries to the shop where Miles keeps his guns. The guns are in a metal cage with the biggest, ugliest lock she's ever seen. The thing is massive and there's no way she can break through it with an ax. A blowtorch will take too long. But...

The cage is like a bunch of chain-link fences welded together. Not incredibly thick either.

Taking no more time thinking, Emma finds an old ax in the far corner of the shop Miles used last year to cut up some wood during an odd cold snap that drifted into the area. The wood heated the shop and office nicely.

Now she hefts the ax and walks to the cage. Her heart sinks a little. If she hits the chain-link cage, won't the ax just bounce off? It...

Her gaze happens on something leaning against the concrete wall near the cage. Emma blinks, lowers the ax and moves toward the object. It's about a yard long and—

She drops the ax. It makes a heavy clank on the cement floor.

"Thank you military agent dudes for distracting him," she whispers and picks up the black plastic gun case, grinning.

She places the case on a nearby worktable and opens it. The gun is the same one Miles used to kill that thing – whatever it was – earlier. She forgets what it's called, and she has only shot a gun twice in her life, but damn it, she needs *something*, right?

After a few minutes of figuring out how to eject the damn magazine, she checks the bullet situation. As far as she can tell it's full. Or at least has enough to take out two guys and a woman anyway. But what if there's more than three...?

She shakes her head. No time to worry about that now.

Another minute to teach herself where the safety is on the rifle, then she storms to the front door. The mutation, or whatever it is, is still scratching. Emma debates about just shooting through the door, then decides to avoid the creature altogether and returns to the shop. Her car is around the back. So, if she exits the shop door and hauls ass, maybe she can get to it before the creature realizes she's outside.

Unless there's more than one now...

Emma opens the walk-in shop door and steps outside.

The night is quiet, save for the rhythmic sea lapping at the beach and dock. There's a slight breeze now, when earlier there was nothing. All the briny, salty smells of the Middle Pacific tumble into her. Almost like a wet Hell. Or something.

There aren't any creatures around and the parking lot is empty. She rushes around the building to where her car, an old thing from god knows when, and got in. She turns the ignition and the beast grumbles to life.

One good thing about having a nearly ancient car…no one wants to steal it. Har-har.

Southbound. She knows exactly where and what that is and speeds toward it, heart a chattering mess in her chest.

CHAPTER 7

"What the shit is this?" Miles walks around the bulky tank-like thing, shaking his head. He stops and looks at Jenna. "Have you seen how big that monster is? It'd swallow us whole in this thing."

Jenna smiles. "That was actually part of the plan. Like a deadly pill. We'd rip out of it, killing the damn thing."

Geri, standing away from them says, "You would not be able to do that. Jörmungandr, her flesh is stronger than anything the earth or man can invent. You would be trapped inside of her until you all died."

Jenna sighs, nods. "And thanks to your…input, we will have to kill it a different way."

Geri shrugs. "Might as well do it right the first time."

Miles slaps a hand on the thick metaled thing, which is no larger than a school bus. "What weaponry does this bastard wield?"

To this, Jenna glances away, obviously in thought, before she says, "Laser rounds. Sonic torpedoes, which shoot two, three times faster than traditional." She gives the tank-like thing a once-over. "Admiral Wade called it a STAV."

"What's that mean?"

Jenna finally returns his gaze. "Submersible Tank Artillery Vehicle."

"Kinky," he says and steps away from the damn thing. "But, unless this thing has delayed laser bursts, we can't use it." He points at Geri. "I need to attach that tooth to one of them, if it's equipped."

Unlike normal lasers, a delayed laser burst has a bullet-shaped cover. Once the burst surges, the bullet cover shoots out first at over two hundred miles per hour. It's this cover Miles wants to attach the tooth on. But only as a just in case situation. His main goal is to find Mike, if he's out there.

Jenna shrugs. "I'm not sure if the bursts are equipped. Ma will know."

"How long before she's set to wake up?"

"In about an hour, I think," Jenna says.

He nods, not wanting to wait, but needing to.

"I'm going to get some fresh air, then," Miles says. "Need to let my brain breathe a bit."

Jenna smiles. "Always the thoughtful one."

Miles pffsts. "I'm just trying not to puke right now." He leaves both women, quickly finds a door to the outside and, once in the salty breeze, shuts the door behind him.

The cloying air only adds to his nausea. He bends over the rails and spurts vomit into the sea.

Two things pop into his mind then. 1) He is at the abandoned Southbound warehouse judging by the fish and sunrise logo engraved in the railing, and 2) How the hell is he going to find Mike in all that open ocean?

There is no answer to the question, however. All he knows is he needs to at least try. Mike is the only family he has.

Once the sick toiling in his gut eases he walks down the narrow walkway, rusting metal creaking under his weight, and to the crumbling remains of the parking lot.

Southbound used to be the epicenter of commercial fishing. Beyond the warehouse is a massive pier and docks for fishermen to unload their hauls. The warehouse then prepared and stored the fish for transportation to various markets as far as Iowa.

Then the sea levels rose. The earthquakes happened, and the world fell off the nutwagon in Crazytown. The fish were still out there, but with more and more monsters slithering out of the fathoms, the populations are dwindling rapidly, making fishing both hazardous and slim to nothing. After a few of the larger commercial boats were capsized due to some monster or another…fishing just stopped all over the Pacific.

The Atlantic still has a good fish trade, but he heard that too is now dwindling.

Earth is dying, giving way to monsters both on land and in the sea. The time of man is depleting.

After a while of walking around and gathering himself, Miles goes back inside the warehouse. It still has that fishy smell, though it's only a faint stench under all the rust. Jenna and Geri are still standing by the STAV, the tank-like sub thing Wade sent them.

Geri grunts and sits on an old, dust laden crate. It groans under her meager weight but holds. She eyes him as he approaches. Those icy, cool blue eyes. Her withered lips curl in what he assumes is a smile.

"You do not believe in any god, do you." Not a question. Geri's gaze holds his attention.

"Not really."

"Why?"

He shrugs. "Would a god let my parents die by a werewolf?"

"Werewolf?" Jenna asks. "What—"

"A hybrid mutant," Miles says. "But to me, it was a werewolf."

"You are referring to the Christian God, I assume?" Geri asks.

He nods, not liking where this is going.

She also nods and leans forward a bit, the crate groaning. "That one is a young god and still exists. She has not fallen."

Miles frowns. "She?"

Geri grins. "The original texts were rewritten to replace SHE with HE in the early days of Christianity."

"Okay. Whatever. So why didn't *she* stop that thing from killing my parents? Why is *she* letting the world turn into a cesspool? For a merciful god, she's not very merciful."

Again, Geri grunts, blue eyes glittering under the yellow light of old bulbs. "Tell me, how would your mind be after you created the modern version of humanity, thinking it will be the greatest evolution since the older gods fell. You give these modern humans everything. Intelligence, talents, art, everything. You give them awareness and self-worth and will. You love these beings. They are your children. Every single one of them and, for a time, they are well behaved children. Oh, there are a few bad ones, but you take care of them easily. Then...suddenly...your children begin turning on you. They forget about you. They replace you with false gods. They fall in love with Lucifer, her brother, that lunatic. They don't believe in you anymore. And for years, you try to convince them otherwise. You try to show them you are watching and you love them. All of them. You try, and they deny you. Your own children. And so, over the centuries, you watch them kill each other in your name and not in your name and just because they want to kill. You want to intervene, but to what purpose? Why stop these beings when there's no stopping them? And you've worked so hard at creating them and fashioning them to yourself, your children, annihilating them is out of the question. Even if you think it might be best, you can't kill your own children. Not all of them because some of them are true to you. Some still believe and love you. A mother cannot hurt her own babies. Not a sane one. And so...you watch and cry and slowly begin drifting into madness."

Geri sighs. "Then you try creating a better human on another planet, but it's not the same. No matter how much more advanced, they are nearly emotionless beings, even if they all love you. So, you abandon them. You return to Earth and see what it has become and you drift away, slipping through different dimensions and not caring about anything. You just drift and forget who you are. You are not a mother. You are not a god. You are nothing. And you drift into oblivion."

Miles, all of this still sinking in, glances at Jenna, who frowns at the old woman.

Finally, Jenna says, "So…our god just gave up on us? And, if he is a she, then what about Jesus?"

Geri, for once, gives a warm smile. A grandmotherly smile. "My dear, she did not give up. She has merely gone mad from all that has happened and languishes through dimensions." She chuckles. "Jesus Christ was her final, true miracle. She is a god and gave Mary the child. That is why Mary was still a virgin. A male god would have had to insert himself, no matter how powerful. Jesus was supposed to be the one who served as proof of her existence."

To this, neither Miles or Jenna say anything. If Jenna is like Miles, he can't think of anything to say. It's so different from what he's been taught.

Miles, still not so sure he believes in the god, but from Geri, he at least might understand why God isn't present anymore, even if she is still around. It's hard to swallow, but makes a bit of sense, he supposes.

"The old gods," Geri says, not looking at either him or Jenna. "They were the vengeful ones. They were the hateful and despicable ones, even Odin and Zeus. You know they were brothers? Odin was Zeus' older brother, but the histories do not recognize this because Odin is Norse and Zeus is Greek. This was actually a decision to split their children. From the evidence I have gathered, they actually got along. They loved each other. But they did not care for humanity much. They were arrogant gods. Boasting in their powers. Only a rare few, all the demigods, in fact, they loved. Hercules, Perseus, Sæmingr, Bragi. These are just a few of the many those two spawned as demigods."

Miles sighs. "So, you're saying we're fucked going up against this creature?" He needs to change the subject because the talk of gods is getting irritating.

Geri blinks. "Jörmungandr is not a full god. It is the offspring of gods and gained god status, though is not a true god."

"But I thought it was a god?" Miles frowns.

"She is. Though not as you might see one."

"What's the difference?"

Geri stands from the crate, dusts off her backside and looks at him. "She can be killed by a human. No matter how tough she is…she can be killed by a mortal with the right instincts. She is a monster god, much like that old leviathan a couple years ago."

"And the only way to for sure kill her," Jenna says, "is to stab her in the eye with that tooth in your pocket?"

"According to my research, yes."

"What if you're wrong?"

Geri looks away from both of them. "Then we shall all die out there."

There are no words. Miles, for one, cannot think of anything to say that hasn't already been said and he's done with asking questions for now.

"The old gods died," Geri says, "and their monsters live."

Not really sure what to do, Miles nods. He's about to tell them they should begin getting the gear ready, when a soft voice floats through the air.

"Well, there he is. Miles Fucking Raine."

He turns, though it takes him a moment to see the small woman standing beside a rusted-out fish counting machine. She blends in so well. Which makes her one of the deadliest of his old team.

He manages a weak smile. "Hey Sylvi."

She steps away from the machine and Miles sees her fully and, for once, all there. The woman has a knack for not showing all of herself to anyone. She's known to hide herself near or behind things. As is her nature.

Sylvi, back in the day, was his assassin. The one he sent in to dispatch guards, mostly.

Judging by how she acts now, she's still as deadly as ever.

"Don't hey me," she spouts. "This is all bullshit."

He shakes his head. "What's bullshit?"

"You being here," she says. "You're not in Dagger Point anymore, remember?"

Taking a line from Admiral Wade, he says, "I'm always a Dagger Point."

The woman chuckles humorlessly. "Yeah? Because the first thing I remember is you just leaving without a word. None of us have even talked to you for three years."

"I didn't know how to get a hold of you," he says. Not a lie. He had wanted to contact his old team many times, mainly just to chat, but didn't have their numbers or physical or email addresses.

Sylvi rolls her eyes. "Yeah. That's what Jenna kept saying."

"It's true," Miles says, making sure there's at least a crate of machine between them at all times. He's seen how quickly she can kill a man. Especially with that sword of hers.

Her gray eyes survey him up and down. "I heard you're a charter protector."

"Something like that," he says and wishes he had a gun. A knife. Anything. His hand keeps drifting toward his belt.

Finally, Jenna intervenes. "Have a nice nap, Sylvi?"

The Dagger Point's main assassin sighs, sits on another wooden crate and says, "Meh. Ma kept talking in her sleep."

Miles smiles. "She still does that, huh?"

Sylvi shoots a cold glare at him. "What do you care?"

"Sylv," Jenna says. "He had his reasons for leaving. You know that."

The woman shrugs. "We all have our reasons, but he could've at least said good-bye."

Despite the tense atmosphere, Miles can't help but feel a bit of pride.

He trained Sylvi in tactical warfare. When she passed the Seals training camps, she was at the top of her class for combat. Coming from a strict Chinese martial arts background aided by her father, Chang Bo, Sylvi already knew how to kill a person before she decided to enter the Seals program. The only thing she hadn't known was how to use guns and to be stealthy. The stealthy part she took to much better than the gun thing, though. In the years that passed, Miles only saw her use a gun once.

Sylvi prefers her sword and knives.

"I'm sorry about that," Miles says. "I should have said good-bye."

Sylvi glares at him for a long time before her face softens a bit. "I still want to stab you in the face."

He chuckles. "You wouldn't be the first."

The tension lessens and he's able to relax a little.

"So, who's this?" Sylvi points at Geri.

The old woman grins. "Your fairy godmother."

Sylvi glances from Jenna to Miles and back again. "Seriously, who is she?"

"Geri Rask," Miles says. "Norse historian and archeologist."

"Among other things," Geri interjects.

Shaking her head, Sylvi says, "They let anyone in these days." She fixes her gaze on Miles. "You see the monster?"

He nods.

"My ancestors would have called it a dragon. But that's not what it is, is it?"

He points at Geri. "She knows what it is."

Geri blows out a long breath, visibly exasperated. Probably wondering how many times she has to repeat herself. "Not a dragon, but close. It is Jörmungandr, brother of Fenrir. Daughter of Loki. She is also referred to as the Mid-Gard Serpent."

Nodding, Sylvi looks at Miles and cocks a thumb at Geri. "You understand any of that?"

"The serpent is a minor god. One of the god Loki's offspring. Fenrir is her brother, and the only thing that can kill her. Something like that. Anyway, we have a tooth."

Sylvi blinks. "A...tooth?"

As if on cue, Geri brings the long, curved fang out from her pocket and holds it up. "Inside this is Fenrir's venom."

"Well, isn't that just lovely," Sylvi says. "But how the hell are we going to kill that thing with a tooth?"

Walking, because his legs are uneasy and need to move or he'll go nuts, Miles says, "Shoot it into Jörmungandr's eye."

One of the woman's thin, dark eyebrows rise. "That…sounds like a fun time. I think we—"

The door behind Miles crashes open. "Freeze! I have a gun!"

He spins, eyes widening, because…he knows that voice. Jenna draws her pistol and levels it on the dark figure on the platform. Sylvi disappears into the oily shadows.

"Miles! Come on!"

He lifts his hands and says, "Settle down Lone Ranger."

Faint, but there, "Huh?"

Miles smiles. "Put the gun down. I'm okay."

"But these…people kidnapped you. I saw it happen!"

He shakes his head. "It was all a ploy to fool someone. Believe me, I wish they hadn't done it this way, but…"

Before he has time to stop her, Sylvi darts out of the shadows, plucks the rifle out of Emma's hands and snugs the blade of her sword under Emma's chin.

"Whoa," Miles says. "She's not an enemy. Stand down, Sergeant!"

Sylvi lowers the sword, though doesn't sheath is, as he had hoped.

"What are you doing here?" he asks Emma.

Rubbing her neck, she tromps down the metal stairs to him. "I thought you were in trouble. Damn."

"I'm not. Sorry about that."

"A lot of sorry's going around," Sylvi mutters behind Emma.

He ignores this, focusing on Emma. "You should go home."

"And do what? Worry about the best damn charter protector I've ever had? Pshh."

He can't help but smile. "Alright." He turns to Jenna. "This is Emma Thomson. She's a biologist and deep-sea diver. I think she'd make a good addition to the team."

"She's a *civilian*, Miles," Jenna says. "How the hell are we going to explain her to the Admiral?"

"I think the Admiral has more important things to deal with right now, don't you?"

After a moment, Jenna nods. "Okay, whatever." She points at Miles. "But she's your responsibility."

"Well," Geri spouts. "You are lovely, dear." She scoots over on the crate and pats the empty space with her hand. Dust plumes. "Come keep an old woman company, will you?"

Emma gives Miles a look he can only assume is bewildered.

"It's okay," he says. "She's our expert."

"That makes it *so* much better, Miles," Emma says, tone seething with sarcasm. "Thanks." But she sits beside Geri and almost immediately, they are deep in conversation.

"She's a liability," Jenna says to him. "You know that, right?"

"She's not going out there," he says. "I just said she's part of the team to calm everyone down. As soon as we're about to set out, I'll send her home."

"I don't think she'll go, dude."

He sighs. "It'll be a struggle, yeah."

"You really *do* let just anyone in these days," Sylvi spouts, appearing beside Jenna.

"Stop it," he says and points at the STAV. "We have other things to think about right now and—"

"The return of Miles Raine," a woman's voice says and Ma steps out of the shadows. At least she's smiling a little.

Miles smiles back. "Hey, Ma. How've you been?"

"Tired," she says matter-of-factly. "All diagnoses of this mission leads to failure, you know."

He didn't, but nodded anyway. Always the factual one, Ma. With her calculations and data. The brains of every operation. Without Ma, everyone would have been dead several times over.

"Well, just so you know." She glances at Emma and Geri. "Who are they?"

Miles laughs, walking away. He can't help it.

CHAPTER 8

In a matter of minutes, Emma knows almost everything.

Geri barely pauses, her thick, Scandinavian accent mottling more than a few words, though not too badly. She tells Emma all about Jörmungandr and her brother Fenrir and how the tooth in her pocket will kill the serpent. She tells Emma of the mission ahead and that the team she's working for is very moody.

Every now and then, Emma's gaze drifts to Miles. He truly is a handsome man, both inside and out. Also, the most frustrating. She kind of wants to punch him in the face right now.

Shit, she thought he was in serious trouble and come to find out he's just hanging with his old Seal buddies. His sorry barely touched her.

Still, she'll help him find his brother, no matter the cost.

Not like she has anything to really lose anyway. No real family to speak of. No children. Nothing but her small charter business. Nothing to get excited about, nor worry. She's known Miles for almost three years. The man has grown on her and she mainly just wants to help. For all the things he's done for her – like save her ass more than once during dives – she feels she should return the favor.

"What are you a biologist of, dear?" Geri asks.

"Marine. All the sea life."

Geri nods. "You might indeed be useful here."

"Thanks," Emma says, not really sure what to say.

"They need someone with some ocean knowledge. So far as I can tell, they are all a bit on the wonky side."

"Okay," Miles says and gestures to Sylvi. "The one who almost cut your throat open is Sylvi." He pats the shoulder of the larger woman beside him. "This is Jenna, my second in command. Over there is, Ma, the brains of the team. And I see you've already met Geri."

Emma doesn't much care for Sylvi's, cold, gray glare, and Jenna appears like she might either fall asleep or break something. Maybe both. And Ma…well, Ma is yawning while tapping away at some device.

Something too oblong to be a phone. Faint beeps sound from her direction.

Geri huffs. "There is two more, yet. Dumb as mules, they are."

Both Jenna and Sylvi shoot glares at the older woman.

"Okay," Miles says and claps his hands together sharply, instantly shattering the tension in the room. "So, the only thing we have is this…STAV? Nothing larger or more powerful?"

"Anything too big and Murdock Jones will ping us," Ma blurts. "His teams would be on us in minutes. Smaller the submersible, the better the chances of slipping by radars."

"And I imagine he'll have, like, dozens of teams out near that location just watching and waiting for us," Sylvi says.

Jenna nods. "This is just like Chile."

Miles grunts. "Almost. Only this time it's a damn army employed by the richest man in America and some monster sea serp—"

"Jörmungandr," Geri quickly corrects.

"Yeah, that," Miles says. "We have that thing and the open ocean itself. Everything is stacked against us here."

"Mmm, not everything," Ma says, brown face curling in a mischievous grin. She lowers the oblong device. "I have equipped the STAV with a cloaking device and jet propulsion. Whatever we can't hide from, we can outrun."

Miles snaps his fingers, as if just remembering something. "Does the STAV have capped laser burst rounds?"

Ma cocks a black eyebrow. "Does a camel live in the desert?"

Miles smiles. "Good. We need to somehow attach the tooth Geri has to one of them."

After apparently thinking this over a moment, Ma shakes her head. "There's no feasible way to securely attach bone to metal."

"Could drill a hole through the cap," Miles ventures. "Stick the tooth through and seal the backside up so we don't lose the laser thrust."

"Could," Ma says, frowning. "The sealant would need to be metal based and strong. A composite, perhaps." She visibly thinks this over, nods. "I need a welder and some iron-based putty."

"On it," Sylvi says and slips away.

Christ, that girl is fast and so damn *quiet*. Like a ninja, or something. Emma isn't really sure what to say or do amongst these people. Miles never really acted so…in charge. So…badass.

Seeing this actually forces a shiver through her. Has he been hiding his true self from her all this time?

"Okay," Miles says. "Ma, you work on the capped laser burst and tooth. Jenna, you and I are going to learn how to run that damn thing.

Few tests in the water before we set out. I want to make sure we know every in and out and glitch."

Jenna nods, straightening a bit.

She likes him, Emma thinks, smiling a bit to herself. *She'll never admit it, but she likes him a lot.*

"Emma and Geri," Miles says, and she almost jumps off the crate. He smiles at her. "I want you two to figure out a good plan of attack if we meet this…Jorumburger."

Geri sighs heavily. "Jörmungandr."

Miles nods. "Yeah, that."

"What about Jakob and Guether?" Jenna asks.

"Those two can sleep for a little longer. We'll fill them in when they wake up." He motions to the large, bulky gray thing aimed for the pool of water where the floor descends. To Emma, it looks like a cross between a big tank and a submarine. "Let's get acquainted with the controls. Ma, you start in on the capped laser burst."

Ma waves him away. "Yeah, yeah. I'll get my drill." She swings off the crate and walks away until the shadows swallow her up.

As the others disperse into their assigned jobs, Geri turns to Emma and places a liver spotted hand on her shoulder. "Do not worry, dear. I already have a plan of attack if we should come upon Jörmungandr."

Emma blows out a breath that's far too heavy to be a sigh. "I don't even know what's going on right now."

Smiling in the most grandmotherly way, Geri says, "Well, we are going to find that young man's brother and kill Jörmungandr, if we have to."

Emma blinks. "Yeah. This is just…so weird."

"Because you did not know this side of him?"

"No. I mean, I knew he was in the Seals and I knew he was a big deal, but he never showed it. He was tough and knew how to protect my clients, but he's never been so…in charge."

"He adapted," Geri says in a soft tone. "That is what warriors do when they return to society. Those who do not go mad, of course."

"Warrior," Emma says, watching Miles climb into the tank-like thing. She guesses she's never thought of him as a warrior before.

Geri nudges her. "He likes you too, I think."

Emma stiffens. "Huh? What?"

The old woman smiles. "Do not think I do not see that spark between you two."

"There's a spark?"

Geri laughs, although it sounds more like a witch's cackle. "Indeed there is, dear. Indeed there is. See it in both of your eyes. I see it even now in yours."

Emma looks away, emotions dueling with each other. Is there a spark? If so, she supposes she feels it from time to time, but usually she acts on her urges. With Miles, she never has, even if she wanted to. Probably because she didn't want to jeopardize the employer/employee relationship. And more recently…friendship. Yes, she definitely considered Miles a friend. Not a very close one because he's always so distant, but still…a friend nonetheless.

Again, Geri nudges her. "Do not worry about it too much, dear. He will come around. You will see. Right now, though, he worries about his brother."

"So, what can I do?"

Geri blinks. "Exactly. What *can* you do? You know sea-life, correct?"

Emma nods. "I'm a marine biologist, yes."

"So, you know a lot about the smaller animals and fish trolling the sea?"

"And temperatures, and plant life. Stuff like that. Nothing that will help with this mission."

"My dear," Geri says, "you will be a great help to this cause." She nods toward the tank-like thing. "Otherwise he would have sent you away."

Emma stares at the open hatch where Miles disappeared into the tank, submarine, whatever it is. "You think so?"

"I *know* so. Now," Geri slips off the crate. "I think we should eat something before we set out."

The old woman shuffles away and after a moment, Emma follows, stomach grumbling.

PART 2: BELOW THE SURFACE

CHAPTER 9

"It's like a standard mini-sub," Jenna says after inspecting the controls.

They stand in something like an airplane cockpit, rather than a submarine control panel. There are two seats and in front of each are horseshoe shaped throttles/steering wheels. A combo he hasn't seen in a long time.

"What the hell did they build this with?" He taps one of the dark monitors set in the panel near the throttle/wheel hybrid. "Spare parts?"

Jenna gruntsnorts. "This thing is like all over the place, dude. Literally half sub and half tank." She looks at him. "You sure you want to take this thing out there? Looks like a deathtrap."

Miles presses a green button in the center of the panel between the throttle/wheels. All the lights blink on. Something above him beeps. "I don't think we have a choice."

"Like hell," Jenna says. "I can walk away from this any time I want to."

He shoots her a firm look. "Then why haven't you?"

"Because of you. I know how much you love Mikey."

Miles chuckles. "He'd punch you for calling him that. Even if you're a girl."

She smiles. "I know."

Of all of them, Jenna has always been the closest. Not in a romantic sense. More like a sisterly way. She used to come to their Thanksgiving dinners years back, even. She knows Mike probably just as much as she knows Miles. She made a good addition to their tiny family. Then, when he left, he just sort of…cut her out.

He sighs. "I'm sorry."

Jenna frowns. "For what?"

"For leaving you like I did. I just…"

She places a hand on his shoulder. "Hey. It's okay. Really. I understand your reasons."

He shrugs her hand off. "Yeah, but you were like a sister to me."

Something in her green eyes changes, though he's not exactly sure what. Where they were once bright, now they're slightly dimmer. "It's okay." She turns to the panel. Beyond this is a curved window. Something Miles is leery of because glass breaks.

The seconds tick by, and finally he says. "Okay. Well, what do you think? Should we give it a test run?"

She shrugs. "Sure. Why not. I feel like dying right now anyway."

He's sure she meant it to be sarcastic, but her tone is slightly off. Deeper. Lower. The sound of a person giving up on something, maybe.

"Alright," he says. "I'll shut the hatch and seal us in. Can you get the oxygen stabilized?"

"I can," she says and says nothing more.

A frown creases his forehead, at least it feels this way. Something is wrong with Jenna, but he's not really sure why unless...

No. She's always been like a sister. And as far as he knew she never wanted him like *that*. Or did she? Does she?

Shit...

Instead of dwelling on it, he hurries to the hatch. Emma and Geri aren't on the crate anymore. He pulls the latch lever, closing it and presses the pink seal button. There's a slight crinkling sound, like a soda can being slowly crushed in a hand.

The pressure is immediate. He struggles to find his breath, moving toward the cockpit area.

"Jenna?"

She's sitting in one of the chairs, face streaming with tears. She quickly wipes them away, sighs, sniffs, and laughs a bit. "S-Sorry." She presses a blue button.

A loud hissing noise fills the STAV.

Gradually, the pressure eases around him. No more does his head feel like it's between steel vises. And his breathing eases.

Once he catches his breath he taps Jenna's shoulder. "Why were you crying?"

But she waves him away. "Thinking about my mom. You ready?"

That's not it, he thinks, but straps into the chair beside her anyway.

Probably best to just let it drop for now. Mike is the main objective and the more time they waste figuring things out, the longer he's out there with monsters.

He just hopes they won't be too late.

Miles finds the land thrusters button to shove the STAV into the water. The moment it splashes though the surface, the damn thing beings to sink.

"Just like a mini-sub?" he asks Jenna.

She wipes away a stray tear and smiles at him. "More or less." Then she taps a wavy icon on the monitor closest to her.

The STAV comes to a sudden halt, jarring Miles a bit with vertigo.

According to his monitor, they are four feet above the ocean floor. It's only forty feet here so…close one.

"You're backup," Jenna says. "I'm the captain."

"I'm cool with that."

Laughing a bit, Jenna nods. "I figured you would be. Now…hold on."

She pulls and turns the throttle/wheel and the STAV and it veer quickly to the right. Before he knows it, they are surging through waters over one hundred feet deep.

"Holy shit," Miles says, "slow down."

"You wanted to see what this baby could do, well…"

She pushes the throttle/wheel in and the STAV dives straight toward the bottom.

Heart crashing in his chest, Miles grips the armrests of his seat. In a moment, the ocean floor becomes visible.

"Oh shi—"

Not at all worried, Jenna pulls up on the throttle/wheel and the STAV levels out at ninety feet.

She turns to him, grinning. "I think it'll do."

"Y-Yeah. I think so. Shit." His heart is a rampaging beast and he wills it to calm down. It works. Barely.

She laughs. "I think you forgot how awesome I am."

"I guess so, damn."

"You wanna try it?"

Miles glances at the throttle then at Jenna. She's smiling. She truly has the prettiest smile. "Um, I think it's best you have it, Captain."

She chuckles and turns the throttle/wheel slowly to the left. High density lights show every detail of the ocean floor, which is mostly sand and trash at this depth. The magnificent coral reefs are all but dead throughout the world. Only a small area near the small island of Australia remains. Once, Australia used to be quite large, but after the sea levels rose…

"You know," Jenna says after a few more minutes and at a depth of three hundred feet, "I think this thing will work."

"Uh-huh," Miles says, bracing himself. "Look out."

In front of them is a small school of hammerhead sharks. Jenna steers swiftly away from them and does a round-about, heading back toward the pier and Southbound Warehouse.

"Yeah," she says. "I think this will work just fine."

They emerge from the water. Jenna switches to land mode and they roll back into the warehouse.

She sets the brakes and says, "Easy as pie."

Miles, heart still thudding heavily, nods. "Uh, yeah." He stands. "I'll gather everyone. We set out in a half hour."

He's about to turn and walk to the hatch at the rear of the STAV when she grabs his arm. He stops, glances at her grip on his forearm and then at her, eyebrows raised.

"I don't think you should bring that woman with us."

"Who? Emma or…"

"Yes. Emma. I'm sure she has a lot of knowledge of the ocean and all, but she really is a liability, Miles."

He huffs out a breath. "You don't know Emma. It won't matter how much I tell her to go home, she's stubborn."

"Just like someone else I know," Jenna says smiling a bit at him.

"Worse. But I'll try. If she doesn't listen, she'll be part of the team."

Jenna releases his arm, chuckling. "Sylvi will stab you."

With a smile and a shrug, Miles turns away. "She's stabbed me before."

Her light laughter follows him through the STAV to the hatch.

It's true. Sylvi has stabbed him before. Not intentionally, that's why it's a bit funny.

They were on a rescue mission in South America. It was night. Sylvi drew her sword as they approached a small encampment where the POW's were said to be held. Miles stopped unexpectedly at a sound and the tip of Sylvi's sword stabbed his right butt cheek. Luckily, he hadn't yelped in pain and blown their position, but it hurt, and he needed stitches once the mission was over. It soon became a running joke among the team.

Apparently, it still is.

He presses the pressure button and opens the hatch. It makes a giant whoosh sound, then he steps out.

"'Bout time," Jakob spouts the moment his boots touch the cement floor of the warehouse. "We've been waiting for like, three minutes, man."

"Yeah, yeah," Miles says, gaze drifting from Jakob to Guether. Both men are sporting all black tactical gear. All ready to go. He smiles and cocks a thumb over his shoulder at the STAV. "Load up. We're setting out in a half hour."

Both men nod and begin packing the STAV with supplies. Water, food, ammo for the STAV and rifles. Miles glances around, but the warehouse is otherwise empty except for Ma working on the cap of a laser burst at the far end. He walks over to her, covering his eyes as she welds.

When she's finished, he says, "We head out in a half hour. Think it'll be done by then?"

Ma slides the welding goggles up onto her forehead and puffs out her cheeks. "Should be. Need the tooth yet."

He nods. "I'll see where Geri ran off to."

"I think those two are stuffing their faces in the kitchen."

"Kids," he says.

She smiles, which is rare for Ma who never really shows much emotion most times. "Agreed. Yeah, get me the tooth and I think I'll have this thing done in time."

"On it." He walks away, heading for the kitchen.

He steps through the archway just in time to see Emma bite into a giant muffin. She notices him, eyes wide, and about chokes on the stuff in her mouth. Bits of muffin spray the table and Geri pats the woman's back.

"Inhaling muffins is dangerous, dear."

Emma sputters, manages to swallow and takes a quick sip of water.

Miles shakes his head. "You really shouldn't be here, Em."

She frowns. "Where should I be, then?"

"Home. You shouldn't be here about to go on a possible suicide mission."

Shrugging a bit, Emma says, "I got nothing better to do. Besides, I need to make sure my star diving protector doesn't run off on me. You're under contract, you know."

He grunts. "Is that so? I don't remember signing a contract."

She waves a hand. "Oh, you did. It's in the file cabinet. You're legally my responsibility, so…here I am." She bites into her muffin, this time chewing and swallowing with ease.

"You will not win this one," Geri says. "You are stuck with her."

Miles sighs. "Yeah. I know."

"What the hell is that supposed to mean?" Emma levels a challenging gaze on him.

"Nothing at all. Just that I know I can't convince you to go home and be safe."

"Damn right you can't," she says, finishing off her muffin and gulping down the rest of her water.

He can't help but smile. The woman is indeed just as stubborn as him in some ways.

Finally, he huffs out a breath, crosses his arms over his chest and says, "Okay, then. I want you to get with Sylvi for some gear. She's about your size and weight, I think."

Emma's eyes widen. "Wait, ninja girl?"

He nods.

"She hates me."

"Probably."

Emma looks away. "Fine. But if she says one derogatory word I'll—"

"Oh, stop it," Sylvi says rushing into the kitchen. "Only thing you'd hear is the swish of my blade." She grabs Emma by the back collar of her shirt and pulls. "C'mon. Let's get you dressed."

Emma gives Miles a wide-eyed "help me" look, then she's yanked out of the kitchen.

Miles sighs, is about to turn and leave the kitchen when he does a double take at Geri. The old woman is grinning. Not just a grin, but a *long* grin. Almost too long to be real.

"What?"

She chuckles. "Young love is the blindest of all loves."

He shakes his head. "I don't—"

She waves a liver spotted hand. "Oh, never mind. Told those two goobers to load my stuff into that sub contraption you have out there. I do not think they did."

Feeling the pressure of time pressing down on him, he crosses his arms once more. "What stuff?"

"Why, the stuff I need for this journey, of course." She leans forward over the table a bit, grinning. "There might be only one way to kill Jörmungandr, but there a few ways to subdue and deter her."

He steps forward, stops. "Really? With what? How?"

"There is a black bag in the next room. Please load it with the other items we are taking, but in plain sight and easy to get to, understand?"

"I got it, but…?"

Geri shoos him away, reminding him way too much of his grandma. He finds the black bag in what might have been the warehouse's lobby. Nothing special, really. Just a black, leather bag about the size of a large purse. But when he picks it up, the thing it like a damn anvil it's so heavy. Something inside clinks as he strains to carry it into the kitchen, avoiding Geri's smile, and out into the main warehouse.

At the STAV, he places the damned heavy-ass bag near the cockpit area. Right by the right-side row of seats. The left row stare at him blankly. Well, if they had eyes anyway.

Jakob and Guether continue loading things into the STAV wordlessly. Air tanks. Diving gear. Inflatable rafts. All the things they need just in case shit goes wrong.

By the time he steps outside of the STAV, Emma, Geri and Sylvi are standing there. Emma, like everyone else save for Geri, is dressed head to toe in black tactical gear. Surprisingly, Sylvi even gave her a pistol, which is fixed to her hip. Like this, Emma looks like a total badass.

"Ready?" he asks.

All three nod. He steps aside as they enter the STAV. Emma doesn't even look at him. After a couple of seconds, he hurries over to Ma. The young woman turns the laser burst cap this way and that. Inspecting the welds, perhaps.

"How's it looking?"

Ma grunts. "As good as it's ever going to be." She looks at him and lowers the cap with the long fang attached to it. "The shot will have to be perfect. No miscalculations."

"I know."

"I'm serious. If you miss, we'll not only lose the fang, we'll be dead."

Miles opens his mouth tell her he knows, then shuts it again. She more than likely knows he knows.

"Alright," he says finally. "Get the cap fixed to a laser blast and we'll set out."

Ma nods. "On it."

"Thank you," he says and returns to the STAV.

A moment later, Ma enters the STAV and goes to work installing the cap to a laser burst.

"So," Jakob spouts, sidling up next to Miles. "How've you been, man?"

Miles shrugs. "Okay, I guess." Jakob is a great kid, but sometimes tries too hard to get Miles' attention. Miles knows how good the guy is in combat and in heart. But sometimes the kid just tries way too hard to gain attention. Especially from Miles. Still, Miles knows how hard of a life Jakob had before joining the Seals, so…

"How've you been?"

Jakob visibly beams. "Good. Well, kind of. I was just integrating into civilian life when this call came."

"Shit," Miles says. "Sorry."

"Psshh," Jakob says. "I missed this shit."

Miles chuckles and pats the young man on the back. "Me too. Let's go kick a demigod's ass. What do you say?"

"I say, hells yeah!"

Once the cap is attached to the laser burst, Ma gives him the go ahead.

"Okay," he announces just outside of the STAV. "This is a rescue mission. Nothing more until it becomes more. We're looking for whatever survivors we can carry from the USS Cutter. And if we encounter the creature responsible, we'll take care of it. This mission is no different than the Arctic Sea Experiment a few years ago. Our primary objective is to find survivors and rescue them."

"And if that big bastard comes at us?" Jakob asks.

"Jörmungandr," Geri corrects, sticking her head out of the open hatch.

Jakob rolls his eyes. "Whatever."

"We have a weapon to kill it, but also, Geri says she has some other tactics to deter the monster," Miles says.

This seems to appease Jakob some, and he nods.

Guether, massive arms crossed over his giant chest, says, "Will the STAV hold many survivors?"

"Only a few," Jenna says, stepping out of the STAV. "But we can call in the Coast Guard for those we can't take on."

"Those bastards never make to time," Jakob spouts.

Jenna snorts. "No shit. But, I can't have them on standby. Murdock Jones might be monitoring their feeds."

"Probably owns them," Guether adds.

"Are we leaving, or what?"

Everyone visibly flinches at the sound of Sylvi's tone. Something brimming with irritation and anger. No matter who you are, Miles knows, you don't piss off a top assassin. Especially Sylvi Bo.

"Okay," Miles says. "Let's move out."

Jakob and Guether pile into the STAV. Miles sighs, gives the warehouse a final glance, and climbs with his old team. He's thinking about Mike as the hatch closes and the pressure inside the STAV pushes into him before Jenna sets the oxygen and stabilizes the bulky, metal tube.

On either side, all the way to the rear, their supplies and gear are strapped down tight. A careful balance Jakob and Guether put together fantastically.

Geri, Emma, and Ma sit on one side of the STAV, while Jakob, Guether, and Sylvi sit across from them. Geri tucks the black bag under her seat the best she can.

Miles stops at Emma, whose eyes are like baseballs in their sockets. She stares up at him, visibly trembling.

"Hey," he says and hunkers down in front of her. "If you can't do this, it's okay. You don't have to come along."

Her eyes close for a moment, and when they open again there's steel in them. The same steel he has admired over the three years he's worked for her. She blows out a breath, inhales, and says, "I'm fine."

He smiles. For someone scared out of their mind, Emma sure hides it well. At least to those who don't know her anyway.

"Ready," Jenna calls from the cockpit. "Everyone strap in."

Miles pats Emma's leg, stands, and walks to the cockpit, closing the door behind him. He plops in the seat beside Jenna, buckles in. "Okay, Captain." He winks. "Let's go fuck shit up."

She grins, rolls the STAV into the water, and hits the thrusters.

A few minutes later they shoot through the dark waters, aiming for the last known coordinates of the USS Cutter.

CHAPTER 10

Geri is snoring, like, leaned back-head lolling as this underwater coffin shoots through the ocean-not a care in the world-snoring. How she can do it is beyond Emma.

How deep are they now? How far out?

It's been about an hour since they set out.

What things are swimming under the surface watching them? Are they being hunted already?

Emma shudders at the thought.

"You're a marine biologist?"

She looks across the way at ninja girl. Emma hasn't learned all their names yet.

Emma nods. "I am."

Ninja girl leans forward a bit, frowning. "Then why are you so fucking terrified of the ocean?"

"I'm…not. Just never been in one of these things before."

Ninja girl laughs coldly. "A marine biologist whose never been in a submersible before." She leans back in her seat. "Interesting."

Emma is about to tell this little bitch that, yes, she has been in a mini sub before when the big man beside her grumbles.

"Lay off her, Sylvi. Jesus."

"Hey, I'm just trying to learn more about our newest team member here."

"No, you're being an ass," the woman on the other side of Emma says. "An even bigger one than usual."

Sylvi blinks, obviously taken aback by the lack of support from her fellow team members.

Finally, she shrugs. "She'll get us all killed. I think—"

"In my experience," Geri says, head still resting back, face turned to the ceiling, "it is the assholes that get the team killed before the inexperienced ones."

If glares could kill, Geri would have been dead in an instant. Sylvi's upper lip curls in a snarl. "And who the fuck are you, again?"

The smaller man sighs, leaned back in his seat and looking away from them all. "Oh, for God's sake, Sylv. Calm your moist nuggets."

"Fuck off, Jakob."

Jakob snorts. "Very original."

Sylvi bares her teeth at Emma and jabs a finger at her. "Stay out of my way and I won't cut you in half. Got me?"

Emma wants to punch her in the face, barely refrains and simply says, "And you stay out of mine."

"Fine."

"Fine."

"Well," says Geri, "now that we got that settled, can we all be quiet now? This old woman needs some sleep."

Sylvi hisses at Geri but brings out a tattered book nonetheless and begins reading.

Beside her, the other younger woman says, "Sylvi likes romance novels. They calm her down. Like anger management."

Emma nods. "I see."

"I can hear you, you know." Sylvi shoots a deadly glare over her book.

"My name is Marertte, but everyone just calls me Ma. And you're Emma?"

She shakes hands with Ma. "I am. Nice to meet you."

"Jakob. But god your memory sucks." The smaller man reaches over to shake Emma's hand.

She shakes his hand. "A lot has happened tonight."

He gives her a firm pump, then releases her hand. "Has been a little crazy, for sure."

"Guether," the big man says, also offering her his hand.

His hand swallows hers, but his grip is gentle, and his shake is not as strong as Jakob's.

"Oh, for fuck sake," Sylvi erupts. "She's not the goddamn Queen."

Everyone ignores her and Guether says, "I know that Geri over there thinks this monster is something mythical, but what do you think?"

"I..." Emma has no idea how to respond to this. She clears her throat. "It must be some sort of mutation." She's banking on all the mutations popping up lately.

Guether frowns. "That's a hell of a mutation, though."

"You are of Norse descent," Geri says, straightening in her seat. "No?"

Guether blinks. "Well, yeah, but—"

"Were you not told the stories of your culture?"

"My parents were Methodists."

Geri chuckles. "No, not religion. Culture. The Norse, or more modernly called Scandinavian, know of the myths. I am sure your parents knew too, though chose not to teach you. Such is the way of most parents who long to change who they are and where they are from."

"Well, Dad talked about Odin sometimes…"

"Ah-ha!" Geri straightens more, obviously excited. "You see! Culture never dies. What did your father say about Odin?"

Guether shrugs. "Mostly about how his grandad told him stories of the Vikings and how our family were once Vikings. Something like that. He only talked about it when he was drunk."

"Vikings…" Geri muses. "A brutal, yet beautiful people. I too am a descendant of Vikings."

Jakob nudges Guether. "Look at you two. When should we expect the wedding invite?"

"Shut up," Guether grumbles. "Anyway, Dad never got much into the mythology."

And so, Geri told the same story she shared with Emma. All about Jörmungandr and Fenrir and their mischievous father, Loki. Though she went a little deeper for Guether than with Emma. For Emma, it had been the bare bones of mythology. With Guether, there are a few more details that add to the Mid-Gard Serpent's power and adaptability. About how, after killing her brother Fenrir, Jörmungandr actually swam into the deepest trench of the Atlantic Ocean to hibernate and mourn her brother, whom she hadn't meant to kill but merely injure. Digging in deep, Jörmungandr fell into a dormant state, kind of like a coma. Yet, somewhere along the line, she got sucked through a passageway as she slept.

When she finally woke, centuries later, she found herself in the Pacific Ocean. A place so alien to her, she momentarily went mad.

Before long, however, Jörmungandr adapted to her new surroundings and embraced them. She fed well, since the Pacific teemed with larger and more abundant prey than the Atlantic. She fed and grew stronger.

Once Geri is finished telling the little story, she leans forward and pats Guether's knee. "I have many stories, if you are interested."

But Guether shakes his head. 'Nope. The Old Country wasn't my thing."

"He's so damned polite, ain't he?" Jakob grins at the big man.

The big man sighs. "Why are you such an idiot all the time?"

"The better to make fun of you with, my dear," Jakob says, laughing.

Guether sighs and shakes his head.

Emma can't help but smile a bit. The two are like some odd, mediocre, comedy duo.

"Nothing to be ashamed of," Geri persists. "Your culture is also mine. True, our ancestors were brutal bastards most of the time, but what culture is not from time to time?"

Guether nods, though says nothing. Still, Emma can see the big man mulling Geri's words over.

Meanwhile, Sylvi ignores everyone, reading her old romance novel. Which is probably just as well. The woman is brash and a complete ass, which makes Emma wonder why. What happened to her that made her the way she is? Bad past? All the shit her and this team has been through over the years before Miles left? Of all of them, Sylvi is the hardest to read. Then again, Miles mentioned she's an assassin. Assassins aren't supposed to be read very well. They hide under one mask or another, or several all at once.

Like most people Emma has known personally. Even her own mother hid behind masks. No one saw her true face until the end of things. Until she was caught having an affair and later shot Emma's dad when he threatened a divorce. Shot him, then bit down on the barrel and blew a softball sized hole out the back of her head. Emma walked into the kitchen the moment she pulled the trigger on herself.

One doesn't know pain until one sees their own mother die in front of them.

Ah, but that's an old pain. One she's buried and rarely thinks about these days. Thankfully she had had good grandparents to take her in and teach her what love was and what morals were. How hard work pays off more often than not.

The point is, Sylvi reminds Emma of her mother a little. The masks…

Beside Emma, Ma is tapping away at some thin gadget. When she notices Emma looking, she shrugs. "I just solved world hunger and a way to filter salt water into fresh water and refill the aquafers."

"Really?"

"Yes. But even so, the Government won't listen to me. They won't even look at my evidence and solutions. I'm cast away like a leper."

Emma frowns. "Why?"

Again, Ma shrugs. "I don't know. Maybe because there are no women in senate anymore."

Emma nods. That might be the sole reason why they won't give her the time of day. No sisterhood in the House. "Sorry. That's messed up."

"It is, indeed." Ma sighs. "But I keep revamping my ideas and solutions in hope they might reconsider." Again, she sighs. "All in vain, perhaps."

Emma places a hand on Ma's shoulder. "Don't think that. I'm sure they'll come around eventually."

"It's been six years since I stood before them."

Emma opens her mouth, then closes it again.

Ma nods. "Exactly."

And the shitty thing is, Ma would need Government funding and backing. She'd need all the i's dotted and t's crossed. Everything would have to be perfect. And the sad thing is, even if she has a solution to save people and return water back into the aquafers, which would solve the draught problem that's been happening for far too long, the Government needs to pass it. Which is an impossible task.

Finally, Emma says, "Good sense takes time." A line her grandma used often, and Emma still finds accurate.

Ma shoots her a bewildered glance, though eventually nods. "Time can change anything."

Emma smiles. "Yes. And—"

The entire vessel vibrates. The lights flicker off, switching to light blue. A sudden sense of motion fills Emma. Mild vertigo. Sylvi drops her book and mutters a string of colorful curse words.

"Whoa," Jakob says. "What the—"

Miles opens the door and presses a finger to his lips. Everyone hushes. Emma almost asks what's wrong, but Guether, apparently noticing she's about to say something, shakes his head at her, frowning.

The forward surge slows so suddenly Emma leans into Geri a bit. The old woman places a hand on her arm, thumb soothingly rubbing. So grandmotherly this action is, it leaves Emma missing her own grandma.

Miles gives her nod she assumes says, "You're doing well. Just stay quiet," then ducks back into the cockpit.

The submersible vibrates again. Steel quietly groans. Then…silence.

Despite Geri's soothing touch, Emma's heart crashes in her chest.

This is it, she thinks. *This is it…*

CHAPTER 11

Over the years, the military has grown lax on enemy threats in the Pacific, Miles knows. The Great Reckoning War made America the supreme superpower as it defeated all who stood in their way. A war that lasted six years, resulting in more deaths than anyone could count. Then came the Civil War II. But that's an entirely different animal.

America got cocky afterward, resulting in what Miles and Jenna are dealing with now.

It's not a sub. At least not a traditional one.

It's something much faster. Something…almost organic by the movements.

And yet, the STAV didn't pick up on any large organic matter nearby. Smaller matter, but nothing large enough to sideswipe the STAV. There are a few pings, showing a relatively large mass messing with the STAV. But if it's a creature, there would be signatures indicating this.

Miles' best guess is an enemy sub of some kind. Something very advanced and moves without sound in the water. Something large and threatening he cannot place, nor explain. Jenna is gaping at him, as though she expects him to tell her what it is.

But all he can do is shrug.

The STAV is shoved drastically again, this time so hard the force rocks him in his seat and a red light on the panel blinks.

"Whatever it is," Jenna says, "it's messing with the thruster stability."

"Well, that's not good."

"Thanks, Captain Obvious."

"I thought you were the Captain." He gives her a big grin.

Jenna rolls her eyes and presses the red, blinking button until it stops, then she turns fully to him. "It's moving too fast. Our sensors can't track it."

"Ma said she upgraded the thrusters…"

Jenna opens her mouth, frowns. It slowly closes. After a moment, she says, "How come she never told me about that?"

"Eh, because you're not the *real* Captain?"

She smacks his arm. Not hard, but enough to sting. "Stop being an ass. How do I engage these upgraded thrusters?"

"We really shouldn't be talking if that's an enemy sub…"

"*Miles.*"

"Okay. Damn." He stands, opens the door and motions for Ma to join him and Jenna in the cockpit.

Ma blinks, but hurries over. "What is it?"

He steps aside, letting her inside the cockpit. She does, although a bit reluctantly.

Once inside, he gives Emma a smile and shuts the door. When he turns, Ma is in his seat, facing Jenna.

"So, um…what's going on?"

Jenna points at the monitor closest to her. "Why didn't you tell me about the thruster upgrades?"

"Ohh, that's what this is about? I thought you'd let me know why the STAV is rocking."

"No idea what that thing is," Miles says.

"Sensors won't lock onto it. It's too fast."

Ma leans over the panel, taps something on the monitor and faces Jenna. "Because you didn't reset the sensors. Now it should—"

A bunch of lights flicker along the panel. A slight, yet frantic beeping sounds.

A moment later, the thing slams into them hard enough to send the STAV reeling a bit. Miles' stomach drops at the extreme sense of vertigo.

The lights flicker again, though this time an image pops onto the monitor with a distance of fifty feet and closing.

"It's…organic," Jenna mutters.

"Probably better attack or hit the thrusters," Ma says.

Jenna grunts, spins the STAV to face the creature and all at once the curved window is full of giant teeth.

"Holy shit," Miles says, bracing himself for impact.

Ma leans back in the seat.

Jenna, tone even, says, "Later gator." She presses the yellow buttons on the handles of the throttles/wheel. Bluish streams cut through teeth, pummel into the gaping mouth.

Miles catches a swirling of blood in the water before the creature snaps its mouth shut and jets out of sight in a flurry of bubbles.

"Damn," he manages.

"So, you think that was the thing that—"

Miles cuts Ma off. "No. That particular monster wasn't big enough."

"Oh," Ma says. "Well, that makes me feel better." Brimming with sarcasm. She glances at Jenna. "Hit the thrusters when I get back to my seat." She stands and walks swiftly out of the cockpit, closing the door behind her.

Miles settles into his seat and buckles in as Jenna snaps her harness on.

"Well, warp drive, Captain?"

Jenna sighs. "I forgot how much of a jackass you are."

Miles laughs as she sets the thrusters to something called High Velocity and looks around a bit.

"What?" he asks.

"Uh, I have no idea right now how to engage the upgraded thrusters."

"I thought you figured this thing out."

"I did. Just not the crazy upgrade Ma installed."

He leans forward, inspecting the panel. "Well, there's gotta be something around here…" An orange button near the monitor catches his eye. He's never seen an orange button on a panel before. "Maybe this?"

He presses the orange button.

The entire STAV trembles. A shrill whine pierces his ears. Then…

Miles is pressed back into his seat as the STAV blasts forward with so much speed every bubble is like a passing star. Long, trailing, disappearing. The STAV's lights do little at this speed and all is darkness in front of them.

They're at two hundred feet, so no real worry about hitting something, but…

He reaches and presses the orange button again. The STAV slows, returning to its normal, steady speed.

"Shit," he manages through breaths.

"Right," Jenna says. "Ma is an asshole."

"She's a genius," he says.

"Geniuses are technically insane," Jenna says.

"Well, she's an insane genius then because…damn."

Jenna chuckles. "That was crazy. How'd she get the thrusters to boost so fast?"

Miles shakes his head. "Shit, I don't know."

Jenna sets the speed to a reasonable one hundred knots and leans back a bit. "We're still on course and should be at our destination in a few hours."

"Use the thrusters," Miles says. "The more time we waste—"

"If I use the thrusters too much, it will deplete the power too quickly."

"The STAV has a nuclear core, so it shouldn't—"

She snaps a glare at him. "Look, I want to find Mike as much as you do right now but we'll be dead in the water for a couple hours while the core recharges. No weapons. Nothing. Anything could come along and crush us."

He wants to hit her, but he also wants to hug her. Because she's right. Sure, they'd make up a lot of time using the high-power thrusters, but, like Jenna said, doing so would leave them drifting two to three hundred feet under the surface unarmed and immobile. Might as well ring the dinner bell.

Jenna stares straight ahead. Not saying anything.

"Okay. Sorry. I just want to make sure he's okay."

"I know. So do I."

"Yeah." He leans back, nudges her arm. "You got this, Captain."

Shaking her head, Jenna looks at him. She's smiling. "Still as corny as ever too, I see."

He winks.

She laughs and pushes the STAV to one-eighty knots.

He's just about to finally lean back and relax when something slams into them. Before he has time to suck in a breath, the world is spinning like an infinite top. As though he's trapped in an antigravity pod. Round and round and…

Jenna, crying out, slams some lever forward on the other side of her wheel. The STAV quickly stabilizes, sending Miles' stomach into a maelstrom. He leans to the side as his equilibrium tries to right itself, about to vomit. Hot salvia fills his mouth, the world is still spinning. Searing bile crawls up his esophagus.

Then, thankfully, everything stills and his stomach eases. The bile creeps back down and he swallows, forcing it the rest of the way. A loud gurgling bubbles in his stomach.

"You alright over there?" Jenna asks.

"Uh…yeah." He kind of wishes she'd be quiet a moment so his mind can catch up to his body.

Still, she laughs. "Guess you should've finished that pod training, huh?"

All over, the STAV is beeping and lights are blinking.

"I didn't need—shush, fix the STAV, *Captain*."

After a few seconds, the beeping stops, and the lights go dark.

"Whatever hit us is already long gone," Jenna says. "Nothing on the sensors. Might've just been a whale."

Miles nods as everything within him synchronizes finally. "Probably." He clears his throat. "Is there a way to, um, scan a few hundred feet out to make sure that doesn't happen again, because—"

The door slams open and Emma wobbles in, face pale and waxy. "Wh-What the *hell*?"

"Whale," Miles says.

Behind Emma, Ma leans in, wiping what appears to be yellowish liquid from her chin. Clearly vomit. "Forgot to mention…there's a feature to detect movement one thousand yards out in all directions."

Miles swallows down more bile. "Hey, thanks for the update."

Ma grabs Emma and pulls her out of the cockpit, then shuts the door.

Miles rights himself in the seat and looks at Jenna. She looks at him.

"Any idea how to engage Ma's feature?" he asks.

Shrugging, Jenna says, "I'll figure it out."

"Hope so. Because that was ridonculous."

Jenna leans forward, inspecting the panel and monitor, not saying anything. And, after a couple minutes, she smiles and taps the monitor. "Found it."

"Well, that's fabulous," Miles says.

"I don't know why she likes to hide things," Jenna says.

Miles shrugs. "She's a genius?"

Jenna gives a firm nod, touches the monitor and his own monitor not only shows the depth, but a complete thousand-yard scan around them. There's nothing within this that's large enough to mess with the STAV. A couple Great Whites, but that's about it.

There's something he remembers Emma saying once but decides to drop it. About whales typically traveling in pods, or something like that. A bunch of them, not just one. So, if they were struck by a whale, wouldn't there be a pod? Or at least a couple others? He dismisses the thought. Maybe they were on the run from something…larger. Something that gave up on them for easier prey, perhaps, since the scans aren't picking up anything larger than the Great Whites.

"At one-eighty knots again. I'll let you sleep for an hour." Jenna sighs. "You probably haven't relaxed for a long time."

The prospect in his mind now, Miles slaps the arm of his seat. "I haven't. Unless you count the drug induced shenanigans you all forced on me."

"We were told to," she says.

"Oh, I know."

Jenna sucks her teeth a moment, then says, "Sleep. I'll wake you in an hour. The seats recline."

Miles finds the lever to recline the seat and sighs relief. To sleep, if only for an hour, would give his mind a restart. It would—

A silvery ping tingles the air. He glances around, fixes his sight on the monitor. In the thousand-yard radius, a large, blue shape emerges. Unlike the Great White images, this one does not so much move, but glide in a straight line toward the STAV. Now at seven-hundred yards and closing.

"It's not organic," Jenna mutters, frowning at her monitor. "Readings are telling me it's made of metal."

Miles straightens in his seat. "What do you need me to do?"

"I'm going to loop around behind them," Jenna says. "Might just be a Coast Guard sub curious about us."

Miles nods.

"If not, the laser cannon controls are installed into these wheels. I've disabled your pilot controls so don't worry about steering. Let's see if they're friendly first."

He snorts. "I remember when I used to give the orders."

She sticks her tongue out at him briefly. "You keep forgetting I'm the Captain in the STAV." She returns her focus to dipping the STAV down another hundred feet and turning. "Now be quiet."

"Aye, Captain," Miles says, smiling a bit.

The laser cannon triggers are on the grips of the throttle/steering wheel. After a little inspection, he finds the symbols. One is of a straight line, the other is an asterisk, indicating a burst, or explosion.

He lightly curls his fingers around the straight-line laser triggers on both grips. The bursts he wants to save, especially since he's not sure where in line Ma placed the only ammo that will kill the giant sea serpent. Whatever its Norse name is or its origin, it's a monster as far as he's concerned. A dangerous one that shouldn't exist. A thing that should not be. And maybe it needs to die. Maybe he deserves to die. If all of Geri's mythology stuff is true, the serpent is kind of a bitch. Creating catastrophes wherever it slithers. People die. Even other gods like Fenrir died by this thing's monstrous nature. And if it killed Mike...

Miles shoves the thought to the back of his mind while Jenna tries to loop around the approaching sub. But...

"Shit," Jenna says through clenched teeth. "They know our movements and are turning. Turning on the cloak. Hold on." She taps a blue icon on the monitor and all the lights in the STAV turn blue.

She changes directions, pulsing the thrusters just enough to make the switch quicker.

The sub, which appears to be somewhere between a mini and a massive war machine, continues following their old direction. The cloak is working. Rendering them virtually invisible. There are hacks to filter through a cloak, Miles knows, but he hopes Jenna can get the drop on them before they figure it out.

She brings the STAV up a good hundred feet, spirals over their pursuers, and drops directly behind the swirling bubbles of something similar to the STAV, only not quite as narrow. And he thought the STAV was bulky, this thing is like a goddamn box gliding through the water.

And...

He squints, leaning forward a bit, focusing through the bubbles on the logo painted on the back of the STAV wannabe. Then his eyes widen. He glances at Jenna and she nods.

"Fire," she says.

Miles squeezes the trigger before he lets his mind stop him. Two reddish beams slice through the murky water into the sub in front of them. Streams of bubbles blow out of the holes and upward.

"Again," Jenna says.

He aims for the armored propellers, squeezes the triggers. Two more reddish beams cut into his target. There's a muffled rumble, black liquid inks the enemy out of sight for a moment or two.

Jenna slows the STAV to a crawl, hissing.

When the black liquid (oil, Miles assumes) clears a bit, the other vessel bobs in the water. Not moving. The streams of bubbles still trail out of the holes in the thing's hull.

Jenna stops the STAV and taps another icon on the monitor. "Before you launch your escape pods, tell your boss to stay away. Every vessel we see, we will destroy. This is your boss' final warning."

A few moments later, eight pods explode from the sides of the enemy sub and shoot toward the surface in a melee of silvery bubbles.

Jenna turns to Miles. "You know who sent that vessel, right?"

He nods. "Murdock Jones. Saw the MJ Oil logo."

"Exactly. He was trying to tail us, which means he somehow knows about our mission."

"Maybe he didn't believe the kidnapping? Maybe he had Admiral Wade tortured?"

Jenna sighs. "Really doesn't matter. He's on to us now and we need to haul ass."

"Well, yeah. I said that before."

She raises a hand between them. "Being a smartass isn't going to help."

"I'm not. I did say to go faster. But we can't risk being sitting ducks. Why do you think I didn't fight you on it?"

She doesn't answer and instead resets their coordinates and increases the speed to two-hundred knots.

A few minutes later, she says, "We're moving fast now. Three hours max before we reach our destination. No thrusters, but pushing her to the limits."

"Good," he says.

"You can sleep now, if you want."

He grunts, smiling. "Yeah, okay. I don't think the imaginary gods want me to sleep anyway."

Jenna reaches over and pats his shoulder. "There, there. Want a tissue?"

Miles laughs. It's a full laugh. Something he hasn't been able to do in a long time.

CHAPTER 12

All Emma knows is she needs to stay quiet. At least that's what Ma told her.

Through all the crazy shifts and turns, now the sub, or whatever it is, is once more moving forward. At least, that's what it feels like. Hard to tell from back here, really, what's going on. But when Ma and the others relax, she soon does too.

She begins rethinking her decision to join in on the mission. Feels like a mistake now and she really doesn't know what good she'll be to these people, or Miles. She's a marine biologist, sure, but what good is that with something out there defying nature? And if Geri is to be believed, they're heading straight for a god, or demigod, or whatever.

Emma shifts in her seat, wanting to stand and pace as her mind races. She…

Geri places a bunch hand on her knee. "Fretting so will not make things better, dear."

"I'm not—"

"You're fidgeting like you have Parkinson's or something," Sylvi spouts, lowering her book.

Emma rolls her eyes but refrains from saying anything to the other woman.

"The blue lights," Ma says calmly, "they mean we're in cloak mode. There was an enemy near, so Jenna and Miles set the cloak." As soon as she finishes, the lights flicker on to clear. "Now we're okay."

"So, what…?" Emma sighs. "We were under attack?"

"Yes," Ma says. "Well, close to it."

"But who would—"

"Murdock Jones," Geuther says. "That rich bastard would have had Miles if we didn't take him."

Emma sees it now. Guether was one of the men that carried Miles to the inflatable boat. Jakob was the other. And in the boat…Jenna? Doesn't matter. They saved Miles from a deranged oil tycoon. Even if their methods were a bit…odd.

"Yeah," Jakob says. "But Miles probably would have been fed better."

"Just when I thought you were asleep," Guether says.

"Man, I never sleep."

"Do too."

"Do not."

"Do—"

"Anyway," Ma interjects. "What do you think this Jörmungandr really is, Emma?"

"Finally," Geri says. "Someone gets it right."

Emma shakes her head. "I don't know. It shouldn't exist, really. Then again, a lot of things these days shouldn't exist."

"So," Sylvi says, "you think it's a mutation?"

Again, Emma shakes her head. "I don't know. It—"

"How come it is so hard for all of you to understand that what we are dealing with is a thing of myth?"

"Uh, because it's a myth?" Jakob chuckles.

"Yes," Geri says. "Jörmungandr is a myth in a sense. All the monsters of old have long since perished or dug themselves deep into the earth to fall dormant. Jörmungandr was one who dug in and slept. She is only arisen and is probably hungry. So she feeds on everything."

"You really believe all that?" Sylvi asks.

Geri nods, smiling. "I do. I have evidence gods and monsters existed in the early stages of humanity. And it will do you all well to know this as fact too. If you want to defeat Jörmungandr, you need to open your minds and realize the mythical world is leaking into ours. Killing a god, even one so minor as this one, takes finness."

"Miles said we might not even encounter the thing," Guether says. "You think that's true?"

Geri chuckles, a sound so much like a witch's cackle it sends ripples over Emma's skin. "Well, it is possible." She sighs. "But Jörmungandr is a resilient being. She's not dumb and running on instincts like most ocean life."

"Most whales are pretty intelligent," Emma says without thought.

"True," Geri says. "Though none of them think like you and I. Jörmungandr does. She is very aware of everything. This is another thing we must all take into account. If we are to defeat her, we must outthink her."

"Bullshit," Sylvi spits, then returns to her book.

Geri sighs heavily, though says nothing more.

In fact, everyone falls eerily silent.

Emma frowns. "How big is this Jörmungandr?"

"Well," Geri says. "It depends on which stories you believe. Some say her body can stretch from the Netherlands to Iceland. The older texts say she can wrap her entire body around the world."

Emma turns in her seat to look at the old woman. "And what do you think?"

Geri sighs, hollow cheeks puffing out a bit. "Realistically speaking, I would guess she's about twice as long as your state of Minnesota."

Everyone blinks at Geri, including Emma.

"Isn't that like eight hundred miles?" Jakob asks, glancing around.

"Eight hundred and fourteen miles, to be accurate," Ma says.

Gaping, Guether shifts in his seat. "How much is that in feet?"

Ma shakes her head. "I'm not even going to calculate that right now. This thing is huge, that's all we need to know."

"Yeah, fuckin' thing took out the second largest battleship in the world," Sylvi says. "I'd say that's big enough."

"Of course, I might be wrong," Geri adds. "There is no hard evidence, only assumptions."

Sylvi grunts. "See. You don't know shit, lady."

"*Sylv*," Jakob says. "That's enough, Christ."

Before Geri shakes her head and looks away, Emma catches the tears wetting her eyes.

Emma snaps her attention to Sylvi. "What is your deal? You have no goddman reason to hate either of us."

Smirking, Sylvi places the book on the floor and leans forward a little. "You ever find a mouse in your kitchen?"

Emma frowns. "I don't know what that has to do with—"

"Shut up. Answer the question."

"Sylv," Jakob says. "Give it a fucking rest."

She ignores him and points at Emma. "I'm talking to her, shit weasel." Her focus never strays from Emma. "Have you ever found a mouse in your kitchen?"

"Yeah," Emma says. "But—"

"And I bet your first reaction was fear. Because it came out of nowhere and startled you, right?"

Sighing, Emma shrugs. "Sure."

"Right. But after the initial shock you kind of thought the little bastard was cute, am I right?"

Emma has never wanted to punch someone so much in her entire life.

"So, thinking this mouse is just the cutest thing ever, you let it live. You don't crush it under your bootheel or set a trap. Nope. Instead you just turn the other cheek and go on about your business. You let it slink off to wherever mice go." Sylvi's smile lengthens into a grin. "A few days later, you open the cupboard to get your favorite cereal and when you pull it out your tasty cereal spills all over the counter. You realize there's a nice big hole in the box or bag, whatever. And when you open the box, there's not only the same mouse in there, but two or three. Now…yes…because you didn't kill it when you first saw it. You let it live. You ignored it. And now it brought in friends. Shit, maybe there's even a few baby mice squirming in the walls now just waiting for their time to crawl out of the hole and tear into whatever goodies you have." Sylvi's grin becomes toothy. "Now you have an infestation. All because you thought a simple little mouse was cute."

After a moment, Jakob chuckles. "So, you think Emma's cute?"

Syvi rolls her eyes. "No, you idiot. I think she's vermin."

Emma begins to stand and Ma quickly pats her leg. When she looks, Ma shakes her head. "She'd kill you before you took a step."

"Damn right I would," Sylvi says, glare narrowing.

Guether places a giant hand on Sylvi and the woman visibly flinches. "Calm down," he says.

Sylvi is about to open her mouth to say something when the cockpit door opens and Miles steps out.

To Emma, he seems a bit on the pale side. Not good.

"We'll be at our destination in about two hours," he says.

Sylvi snaps her glare at him. "What the hell was all the turning and shit going on about?"

Miles, pinching the bridge of his nose with the index finger and thumb of his right hand says, "MJ Oil. Murdock was tailing us."

"Well that horse's dick," Jakob spouts.

"How did he know about us?" Ma asks. "I took strict precautions so he wouldn't."

With a shrug, Miles says, "I don't know."

Emma stands, about loses her balance from all the momentum of the vessel and braces herself to against the wall. The metal is cold. She nods at Sylvi. "She's being an ass to both Geri and I."

Sylvi, all wide-eyed. "Well, of *course* I am."

Miles, still pinching the bridge of his nose, says, "Sylv, chill. Geri and Emma are here for a reason."

"She told them the mouse story," Jakob says, chuckling.

Miles sighs, shakes his head. "Sylv, that's an old story."

"It's a *true* story."

Hand finally straying from his nose, Miles waves the hand. "Whatever. Play nice. They're both good people here to help."

"And what the fuck are they supposed to do? Neither of them know how to fight." Sylvi points at Emma. "Bet Ms. Princess has never even fired a damn gun."

"And what the hell does that have to do with anything?" Miles says, voice louder. Not quite yelling, but close.

Sylvi frowns. "Means she's worthless to this mission. I really don't care what she knows about the ocean. How the shit is that supposed to help us?"

Miles levels his glare on Sylvi. "Do you know about the temperature of the water where we are right now, at this depth? Do you know what predators we might encounter at this depth? What about the climate tides?"

After a few stubborn seconds, Sylvi lowers her eyes, looking at the floor. "I doubt she does."

"Okay," Miles says, "fine. Emma, we're about one thousand miles off the coast at a depth of three hundred feet. What's the average temp in these waters?"

Without thought, Emma says, "Around fifty degrees. Maybe forty."

"Why are we only at three hundred?" Ma asks.

"It's a depth Jenna is comfortable with." Miles never stops looking at Emma and his heart flutters a bit.

"We should be at three hundred *yards*."

But Emma shakes her head. "No. Three or four hundred feet is ideal here. If I remember correctly, there's a rise in the ocean floor coming up. If we were in yards it'd create a problem."

"So," Sylvi says, "You're saying you have no idea what you're talking about? Because apparently Jenna already knows."

Emma, fists clenched at her sides, tries to ignore the woman. She makes sure Miles is paying attention. "We should ascend to one hundred feet below the surface to avoid the shelf coming up."

"How much longer do we have?" Miles frowns.

She shrugs. "I have no idea, really. But you said we're about a thousand miles out and the Outer Pacific Shelf is about that distance."

"Fuckin' earthquakes," Jakob says. "Creating ocean shelves and shit."

Miles rolls his eyes, looks at Emma. "You're sure about this?"

Laughing humorlessly, Emma shakes her head. "No, but better safe than sorry, right?"

He nods. "Right."

"Anything one hundred feet and above is detectable," Ma says.

"Even with the cloak?"

Ma slaps a hand to her forehead. "Why...why am I stuck in a STAV with simpletons?" She lowers her hand, gaze fixing on him. "The cloak won't matter that close to the surface. We can be easily pinged and our progress through the water tracked. Anyone looking will see us."

Emma hadn't considered this and wants to kick herself for being so stupid. She blows out a heavy breath. "Keep us at two hundred then. Just keep an eye out for variations in the floor. There's the Shelf, but there are also sunken ships and god knows what else."

Miles smiles and her heart tumbles in her chest. She always liked his smile.

There are so many ways to be attracted to someone, other than the physical, Miles had the physical thing down, but he's deeper than that. Much deeper, Emma is coming to find out. His smile is slightly crooked, but in a way that's endearing rather than strange. His dark, brown eyes hold old ghosts in them. Ghosts she noticed from time to time when he looked at her, though never asked him why. They're haunted eyes. Eyes that have seen more than most people should. Eyes that watched people die and witnessed horrors far worse than any monster roaming on land or gliding through the seas. But they are also eyes of patience and kindness.

It's what's behind those eyes Emma is more curious about. Beyond all the physical bullshit. Miles can be an ass, yet at the same time, he's the sweetest man she's ever encountered in his own quiet way. It's like there's a duel going on inside him constantly. Maybe there is.

Not like she'd ever ask him about it, but still…it's this mystery which attracts her more than his crooked little smile. What secrets does he hold within him? It's not about wanting him, though more about knowing him.

He shuts the door, returning to the cockpit.

"Well," Jakob says. "That was fun." He turns his attention to Emma. "Marine biologists know about geography?"

"Not really. I did some research a while back because I was bored."

"Wait, wait, wait," Jakob says, standing. "Hold the jelly. You were bored so you…studied the geography of the ocean?"

She sits, chuckling and not able to stop herself. "It's what I do on vacations too."

Jakob blinks, then gapes at her. "You're like one of those prodigies, aren't you?"

Emma, chuckles forming into a laugh, shakes her head. "God no. I just like learning things."

"For shit sake," Sylvi grumbles. "You two wanna get a room?"

He points at Emma. "She's just sour because you like me better."

Picking up her book and opening it, Sylvi grunts. "She wishes."

Guether sighs heavily, leans forward and rubs his temples with his thick fingers. "This is gonna be a long goddamn ride."

Jakob and Emma look at each other, then both burst out laughing.

CHAPTER 13

His lips press against Emma's, and oh god she tastes so good. He pulls her closer and…

"…all this?"

Miles, emerges from the dream, blinking at the ceiling of the cockpit. "Huh?"

"I said, are you seeing all this? What'd you do, pass out on me?"

There have only been a few moments when he actually wanted to strangle someone. This is one. Still, he sits up and squints at the ocean beyond the cockpit. He told Jenna to keep the depth at two hundred feet maximum and now they find themselves in a shipwreck graveyard.

Emma hadn't been kidding. How a marine biologist knew about this is beyond him, nor does it much matter. Because…

"There's the USS Reaper," he mutters.

"I lost two friends when it went down," Jenna says.

He nods. "I know. I remember."

They pass over the Reaper and Miles is struck by all the death spanning before him. Ships frozen in their underwater graves for all eternity, or until they rust into nothing anyway. Which, judging by most, nothing is approaching. And yet…

"That's not…"

Jenna gasps. "Oh my god, it's a pirate ship!"

Not really sure what to say, he nods.

Jenna asks the question building in his mind. "How is it still even intact?" She slows the STAV so she can really look at the ship. "Wouldn't wood break down?"

"Yes. Unless…it fell into a deep trench and spat out on the Shelf when the earthquakes happened." Miles shifts in his seat. "If there were still museums they'd pay millions for this ship."

The ship is blanketed in barnacles and various small corals. All green and mossy looking in some places, even though he knows that's not moss. It's life living off death. Life breeding on the skeletons and creating something new.

As they drift over the pirate ship, Miles' gaze latches onto a human skeleton half in and half out of a door in the deck of the ship. It's covered in barnacles as well, though still very much identifiable. A pirate, probably as the ship was sinking, woke up and tried escaping the ship. Maybe his pant leg got snagged on a nail. Maybe he was hurrying so much he tripped and cracked his head on the deck hard enough to knock him out. Whatever the case, he died as the ship sank.

Jenna expertly maneuvers through the shipwrecks.

"Why are they all in this spot, though?" Miles asks.

Jenna huffs out a breath. "Maybe the earthquakes and everything stirred them all up here?"

It makes sense. Unless this is a focal point of attack by...something...

And if so...what?

If there's something out here that sunk these ships, it has to be one aggressive, mean bastard.

Then again, that's all speculation. Maybe the quakes fucked everything up. Sucked ships from other locations in and spat them out on the newly formed Shelf. It's possible, he supposes.

It's also very possible there's something big stalking these particular waters.

He checks the thousand-yard scan. Nothing but a school of some fish or another and what might be a pod of orcas since humpback and grey whales and dolphins have been extinct for a dozen years or so now.

Nothing large enough to destroy anything.

The graveyard stretches on and on and after a while, he wants to tell Jenna to speed back up. He's had enough of this shit. They are on a mission and ogling over fallen ships is just wasting time.

But he stops himself from giving the order. Jenna is no doubt thinking about her friend right now. She needs a bit of time.

So, he once more leans back in the chair. Just before his eyes shut, he says, "They're still heroes."

He falls asleep before she responds.

When he wakes some time later, Jenna is singing some song to herself.

He rolls a bit to look at her. She steers the STAV and, smiling, as she sings, "Dead, they all fall down. I have...this thundering sound. Of power, against all man."

He's not sure if he has ever heard that song before, but it sounds familiar.

"Unload," Jenna sings. "Unload and reload, all of 'em, like putrid toads."

The name of the song still refuses to surface in his mind.

Once her singing begins to lull, Miles says, 'How long was I out?"

"Dying in—oh, hey, welcome back. Been about an hour."

"How much closer until we get to our destination?"

"Should be an hour," Jenna says. "Give or take."

Ahead, through the glass of the STAV is nothing but dark water. At least as far as the lights reveal anyway.

"How was the graveyard?"

Jenna shrugs. "Once you see one pirate ship, you've seen them all."

He adjusts his seat so he's sitting upright. He's still tired, more than a little thirsty and needs to take a piss like no other right now. Bladder swelling, he stands. "I'm gonna take a leak. You okay here?"

She waves a hand at him while she studies the waters through the windshield and the scans on the monitor.

Miles hurries out of the cockpit and into the main body of the STAV. Emma is asleep, head resting on Geri's shoulder. The old woman gives him a small smile as he passes.

"It's a tight fit, bro," Jakob calls after him.

He doesn't respond. He knows what the head looks like in the STAV. Something more like one of those ancient telephone booths than a bathroom at all. Even a tighter squeeze than the old latrines Colonel Ramson made them build during the Marine/Seal crossover thing everyone thought would be awesome, but never was. The project, to merge both branches, proved to be a disaster. Tempers ran too hot. No one worked as a team, no matter how much the Colonel roared at them to do so. There was respect among the branches, but that only went so far. Eventually the project was scrapped and both branches returned to their usual routines.

One thing both Marines and Seals agreed on, however, were the narrow latrines.

Miles squeezes into the STAV's tiny bathroom, finishes his business while each shoulder presses against the wall and shut door.

Sighing, he opens the port to let the urine splash into the waste tank. "Whoever designed this smoked too much crack," he mutters to himself and steps out.

The team are all seated, none of them talking. Geri, head cocked at an odd angle, begins to snore. Emma leans over, checking out whatever Ma is tapping at on her tablet. Sylvi is reading. Guether is picking at his fingernails with the tip of his knife and Jakob…well, Jakob pulls out a small wad of snot from his nose and wipes it on the side of the seat.

Miles stands between the two rows of seats, wanting to say something. Anything, really. But no words form. All he can do is glance at each of them. His mind buzzes with possible ways to motivate them and boost morale, and then flicks each away one by one. When all he feels is trepidation and the growing need to find his little brother, all that shit strips him of any speech.

So, instead, he nods and returns to the cockpit.

"That was the longest piss in the history of pissing," Jenna says as he shuts the door.

"I had to turn into a pretzel to get into that…whatever you want to call it."

"It's called the head, but I guess closet works too."

He plops down in the seat beside her. "I want to punch whoever designed that in the nuts."

Jenna snorts, then bursts into laughter.

He smiles, leans back in his seat and stares out into the endless ocean.

His thoughts soon turn to Mike. His little brother. All he has left of his family.

It's been, what? A few days since the serpent sank the USS Cutter? Something like that. If Mike is still alive, he's most likely in a raft or one of the pods. Although, maybe not a pod because all pods are programmed to locate and depart to the nearest land mass upon being deployed. So, unless the pod Mike got into was damaged in some way, he's more than likely on a raft, which is a last resort during a sinking.

"About a half hour now," Jenna says. "But you know he's probably not near the area anymore, right?"

"I know," he says, still staring out the curved windshield. "We'll begin our search from ground zero."

"That might take a long time, Miles."

He snaps a glare at her and she visibly flinches. "I don't care. Whatever it takes." He stares out the windshield again and repeats, "Whatever it takes."

He feels her gaze on him like two hot spikes piercing the side of his face. Ignoring this as best as he can, he mutters, "We have to try."

"Miles," Jenna says, tone very low. "We *are* trying."

Sometimes life shits on you, Miles knows. Sometimes it chews you up and spits you out in a wad of greasy flesh. Sometimes it's like a little kid tapping your forehead with a small fingertip. Not necessarily painful, but annoying as all hell. But sometimes…it gives you a break. Life backs away and allows you to actually breathe for a moment.

All Miles is looking for is that breath. Just one tiny breath.

A while passes and Jenna says, "We're here."

He glances at her, then out the curved windshield. It doesn't take long to spot the USS Cutter.

The ship is massive, yes. Huge. Yet its hull is so mangled it gives Miles a very real idea what kind of monster he might be dealing with.

Jenna steers the STAV toward the battleship for a closer look. And no matter how much he wants her to begin the search, he's curious. The closer she gets, the more details come to light and he kind of wishes they hadn't.

A couple of hammerhead sharks circle the wreckage, though dart out of the way as the STAV nears.

"My god," Jenna whispers.

Miles leans forward while Jenna maneuvers the STAV even closer to the hull. Mangled isn't the right word. Decimated might be closer. It had literally been ripped apart. And the more Miles studied the massive hole, the more he noticed the tooth marks and deep gouges in the metal. It's like this thing simply came up and bit a hole into the ship. And it's not the only hole. There's also one, much larger, in the bow. Not only this, the ship appears to have been twisted, making Miles think about how pythons constrict their prey and crush them to death. The image is a nasty one, so he shoves it away quickly.

He's about to look away and tell Jenna to send out two-mile pings for anything on the surface when something thumps against the STAV's windshield. Jenna gasps.

The body, held by the movement of the STAV, does not slide off and Miles gapes directly into the scarlet, empty eye sockets of a woman. Some of her face is missing, possibly chewed away by sea life. She finally slips off the windshield but another body floats from the wreckage. This one a man. One of the hammerheads swings around, darting toward the body.

Before the dead man can reach the STAV, the shark snags him by the leg and rags him out of sight.

"Get us away from here," Miles says, choking down a hard lump in his throat. "Send out two-mile pings."

"Yeah," Jenna says, her voice barely audible. "Sounds good." She moves the STAV away from the wreckage and propels it a few hundred yards away. She presses some button and faces Miles. "Pings four miles out are being sent."

"You can do that?"

Jenna levels a look on him. "Are you really that stupid, or just pretending?"

"Guess I'm that stupid. Last I knew we could only ping two miles out."

She chuckles, claps a hand on his shoulder. "Times have changed, old man."

"Heh, apparently."

"Don't do that."

He frowns. "Do what?"

"Don't say, 'heh', you sound like a grandpa."

He waggles his eyebrows. "Maybe I am."

Jenna laughs. "Doubt it. You can't even stay in a stable relationship for more than two months."

"I...*heeeyyy*..."

She laughs a bit more. "Well, it's true. Anyway, be quiet so I can hear the pings when they come back. You're seriously messing with my mojo here."

"Since when do you have a mojo?"

She swishes a hand at him. "Shut up."

In a military situation, she'd be up for a report for misconduct. Here, though, all Miles can do is smile. He doesn't say anything more and waits for the pings to reveal something.

No doubt Murdock's men are near and keeping watch, but when the pings come back, he's surprised. There are no ships or vessels of any kind for four miles. But...

He taps his monitor. "What's all this?"

"Looks like minor debris," Jenna says. "Almost three miles out. But we'll go look."

While she sets the coordinates, Miles' heart quickens. Maybe Mike will be amongst this debris. Although, being only three miles away feels unrealistic somehow. The ocean has currents after all, like a vast river. Realistically, Mike could be anywhere by now. Still, Miles holds out hope, as one does, his brother will be amongst the wreckage.

The STAV closes the distance and—

"Life forms," Jenna mutters.

He frowns at his monitor. Six heat signatures pop out of all the blue and gray images. "Human?"

"Looks to be," Jenna says.

A sense of triumph spills through him. "Let's check it out."

"We'll risk being seen, though."

Miles thinks this over, and after about a minute, he says, "Do it."

Jenna sets the depth to SURFACE, as pointed out on his monitor and the STAV floats upward.

Fidgeting in his seat, he wishes the damn STAV would rise faster. All submersibles are always so slow at surfacing. It's a safety thing, he knows, but shit...

Once they breach the surface, Jenna says, "You can go up and see what's going on now."

"Can't I do it from here?" Miles asks. "I mean, in case we need to dive?"

"There's nothing major showing up in the thousand-yard radius," Jenna says. "I think you're okay for now."

Not thinking, simply moving, Miles bolts out of his seat, finds the ladder in the cockpit and says, "Open it up."

There's a loud whooshing noise and the small hatch pops open as he climbs the ladder.

He has no idea what to really expect, but old lessons die hard. Trusting the gut is often better than trusting a computer. Human instinct is a powerful thing. Seeing with one's own eyes solidifies belief. It's something he's always known, but Jenna reminded him of. Three years away has really messed him up.

The wind outside wheezes across the hole above him and when he climbs to the top and peeks his head out, he's assaulted by the salty air. Miles coughs, tries to take shallower breaths to allow his lungs to adjust to the salt laden winds. Then he pulls himself up and sits along the edge of the hole into the STAV. It's morning and the skies are flawlessly blue, the sun a massive ball of angry heat already baking into him. One thing he misses about the Atlantic are the more reasonable temperatures. Nothing as scorching as it is out here. In fact, it's almost comfortable on a majority of the Atlantic. Well, until you venture south, then things get choppy and nasty with all the massive waves and constantly shifting weather. Snow to rain, sun to ice.

Water slaps the sides of the STAV. Seagulls cry, circling above. God, he hates those fucking things.

Squinting against the glaring sun off the water, Miles' heart stutters.

For a moment, he can't find the words or voice to express anything.

Then…

"Shit."

For, floating all around the STAV were bodies. Many of them are wearing lifejackets, though some aren't. The latter float either face down or cloudy eyes staring at the sun. The rest bob with the small waves, heads lolling.

As he gapes, a seagull swoops down, lands on a nearby corpse, and stabs its beak into his eye. A second later, the bird yanks the dead man's eyeball out and hops to another corpse to swallow it down.

Rage, unlike anything he's ever felt before, explodes through him. He pulls the pistol from the holster on his hip, aims at the seagull and squeezes two rounds into the fucking bird. It squawks once before flapping into the water, soon dying.

Miles stands on top of the STAV and inspects each corpse he can as Jenna propels the vessel slowly through the horror show. None of them, so far, are Mike, which leads to a spark of hope. Still, he carefully looks at every face, besides the ones face down in the water. Once they are through the swath of corpses, a shiver scuttles through him like tiny, black spiders. There are so many. All this life just…gone. And all of them no doubt died of exposure to the deadly sea. In a way, maybe it would have been better to go down with the ship or eaten by the monster that sank them in the first place. Why the damn thing hadn't swallowed them up is beyond Miles. Maybe all it lives for is to destroy things, not consume. Why would a demigod eat people anyway?

Finally, Miles climbs back into the STAV and Jenna shuts and seals the hatch.

He drops into his seat, staring out the curved windshield.

"So," Jenna says. "What'd you see?"

He draws in a breath, lets it out slowly and shakes his head. "Death."

"What do you m—"

"Just…go."

Jenna says nothing more and speeds the STAV up to sixty knots.

Miles shakes his head, sight drifting to the returning pings, hoping he'll find Mike alive.

CHAPTER 14

She's had enough.

Emma stands and makes her way to the cockpit door.

"Um," Jakob says. "Us lowly pawns stay out of the cockpit, hun."

"Well, *hun*," she says. "I need to know what's going on."

Jakob uncrosses his arms and sits up straight. "We all do. But Miles and Jenna will let us know when we need to know."

"I really don't care."

He chuckles. "Well, it's your funeral."

"Sit back down," Sylvi spouts, not looking up from her book. "Or I'll cut that pretty face of yours off and feed it to the sharks."

Emma rolls her eyes, opens the door and steps into the cockpit. When she turns to shut the door, Sylvi reaches out and taps a blade on her cheek.

"You need to learn that I don't fuck around," Sylvi says.

Sneering, Emma says, "And you need to learn to back the fuck off." She shoves Sylvi's hand away and slams the cockpit door.

"The hell?" Miles stands from his seat.

He doesn't look well. His eyes are too bloodshot and his skin too waxy. In fact, he looks like a gentle shove would knock him over.

Emma cocks a thumb over her shoulder. "You need to talk to that woman. She's fucking nuts."

Miles frowns. "Who?"

"Sylvi. She's threatened my life more than once. This time she touched me with her knife. On my *face*."

Jenna grunts. "Lucky she didn't slit your throat. I'd say she likes you."

"*What?*"

Miles nods. "Sylvi kills people she doesn't like. If you're not dead yet, then she likes you, no matter how much she complains or threatens your life."

Emma's gaze drifts to the curved windshield, then back to Miles. "Well, that's fucked up."

"It is. But that's how Sylvi works."

Emma crosses her arms over her chest. "So, what's going on?"

He looks away. "We're still searching for Mike. You can go sit down now."

"No. I mean, where in the ocean are we? Why did we slow down so much?"

"Look, I—" Miles begins and Jenna cuts him off.

"We're just fifty yards from the location of the wreckage. Middle Pacific, approximately three thousand miles from shore."

This information clicks through Emma's brain. Then she flashes a glance at Miles. "Have you found the Western Slope Current yet?"

"The Western...what?"

"Western Slope Current," she repeats, brushes by him and sits in his seat. She can almost feel his bewilderment boring into her. She tries ignoring this and continues. "It's the strongest and deepest current in the Middle Pacific, though only mild on the surface."

"I...*what?*" Miles sounds so damn confused and she can't understand why.

"Okay, so if the Western Slope flows through the site of the wreckage, whatever was expelled from the ship will be carried away by the current."

Standing right beside her now, Miles says, "So, what are you saying?"

"The deeper it is, the stronger the current. I'm saying, if we follow the current, we'll find whatever has been expelled from the wreckage."

Miles blinks. "So, we're going the right direction?"

"Yes." Excitement wells inside her. "But I'd stay closer to the surface and speed up a little. I don't know how long it's been since your brother's ship sank, but I'm guessing if he's in a raft he'll be a few miles out, drifting on the current."

"Where does the current end?" Jenna asks.

"It goes all the way to China. If Japan hadn't flooded over with the rising waters, that'd be the place we'd shoot for. So, look to China as a final destination."

She catches a smile from Jenna, but Miles' frown deepens. It furrows his forehead and she fights to wither under his gaze.

"You think Mike might be on this current?" Miles breaks the withering look and turns to the windshield.

"It's the logical solution."

After a long time, he finally nods. "Okay. So, we'll follow the current and see what we can see."

Emma smiles, feeling like she actually contributed to the cause. "Make sure you stay close to the surface. Ping several times."

He nods and places a warm hand on her shoulder. "We'll do that. Thank you."

She pats his hand. "I'm here to help. Never forget that." Then she stands and walks to the door. She gives him a final look. "The ocean is unpredictable, but I think this is the right course of action. Stay on the current, and we might just find Mike."

Then she opens the door and steps out of the cockpit.

Sylvi is reading her book and doesn't even look up when Emma returns to her seat. Jakob smiles. Guether continues parring his fingernails with his knife. Ma taps away on her tablet while Geri snores.

No one says anything.

And so, after about living in ten minutes of silence, she falls asleep on Geri's narrow shoulder.

CHAPTER 15

"She's pretty knowledgeable about the ocean," Jenna says. "And not just marine life."

Miles shrugs. "Maybe she studied more?"

Jenna nods. "Maybe. The main question is: Do you believe her?"

"I do." Why Jenna would ask such a question is beyond him. Emma is always very factual. Then again, Jenna doesn't know Emma either. "She's been right about a lot of things."

Leaning back in her seat, black eyebrow lifting. "Oh, yeah? Like what?"

"Not on this mission. I mean over the three years. She knows certain things about the ocean and its currents since all the quakes. She knows how everything has shifted not only on land, but in the oceans too."

"Okay..." Jenna says. "But that doesn't give me an example."

"Alright. Fine. We had some clients that wanted to explore the fairly new Wyright Reef. Emma warned them against it. The ocean floor is unstable, she told them. Variant temps. From scalding hot from all the leaking magma to near freezing. And...somehow she just knew there might be mutations skimming the waters. But those yuppies fed her more and more money until she finally agreed. She took all precautions. Gave us all anti-temp suits to adjust to the fluctuating water temps. I chose an AT-13 sonic round rifle. The clients didn't believe her. Neither did I really. It was our fourth outing and I hadn't really gotten to know her yet. She was just my boss at that point and not a friend." Miles sighs. "So, we arrive at the dive spot. We set the thrusters to keep the chatter in the same location and jump in. We're not even seven meters down when we're attacked by a mutation. This long, eel-like thing with multiple mouths and webbed hands. I dispatched it as quickly as I could, but not before it snagged onto a client and took her for a short ride. There were more, but I set off flares that kept them away. Emma led the way toward the reef and soon enough, more than a few clients were asking to return to the boat. Around twenty meters, we experienced the fluctuations in water temps.

Very cold to extreme heat. A heat even Emma's special suit couldn't stop. The clients pleaded to go back and, finally, Emma gave the order to return to the boat. They settled on the safer and established Gornali Reef south of the Wyright. She was right about everything and after that, she was right about everything else concerning the ocean. Besides the mutations, which is my expertise."

Jenna, nodding, doesn't say anything for a moment. She's in thought, he knows. Has all the signs. The distant expression. The way she sucks on her top teeth the tiniest bit. The slight line forming between her eyes.

Finally, she straightens and says, "So, you two are just friends?"

He flaps his arms in exasperation. "Out of all that, the only thing you heard was that we're friends?"

"No, I heard it all. You two just seem very close."

"It's a business friendship. More or less."

"More or less," Jenna muses, grinning. "You *like* her."

"I—what? No. I mean, yes. But not—"

"Oh, shush. Doesn't matter. If you trust her, then I will too."

He lets out a breath of relief. "Good. She might seem fidgety and awkward, but she's a good person, strong and knows her shit."

"Good enough for me." Jenna returns her attention to piloting the STAV and checking pings.

So far, nothing has shown up on the pings.

Miles debates going back and maybe chatting with Emma a bit, show everyone just how great, if not badass, she can be. Instead he sits and watches for pings.

A heavy sigh leaks out of him and he's about to tell Jenna to gun it a bit when—

A series of shrill beeps nearly force him out of his seat. The image on his monitor shows several different objects on the surface.

"Larger than the last," Jenna says. "Could be rafts or stalled pods."

"Go," he says, heart stammering. "He might be here."

Without a word, Jenna surfaces the STAV. Miles hurries to the top hatch and begins climbing before she even has time to open the hatch.

This is it, he thinks as the hatch hisses open and the salty air whooshes down the hole to him. Once more, he coughs, though not as bad as last time. It's been a while since he's been in the open ocean and all the saltiness of the air. Then again, one never really gets used to that either.

He climbs to the top, pulls himself out and looks around, Mike's name already flirting with his lips.

But what he sees isn't anything he had hoped.

There are rafts. Four of them. And a single pod. All drifting along the current. But...

He stands on top of the STAV, inching his way close to the right side.

None of the seamen move. And one of the rafts...there's only two whole bodies. The others appear to have been slaughtered and...eaten.

Miles shakes his head. No, it hadn't been long enough for them to resort to cannibalism, yet, there's no denying what he saw. Slathered all over inside the raft is blood, now dried to a deep crimson. There are also a few limbs. A ragged arm. A couple of legs. A...head.

Hot saliva squirts into his mouth. His stomach froths, and he spurts vomit onto the STAV. Once the nausea passes, he focuses on the floating pod.

Without really thinking, he shouts, "Hello? We're here to rescue you!"

None of the bodies in the rafts move. None of them are Mike either. But he notices slight movements through the pod windows.

Through the hole, he yells at Jenna to move the STAV northwest ten meters.

The STAV soon putters toward the pod. About twelve feet from it, he tells Jenna to cut the thrusters. The STAV drifts to the pod, bumping into it.

Miles scrambles over the roof of his vessel to the pod, leaning to peek through the window. The glass is too thick and he can't see through it clearly, but as far as he can tell there are three people inside.

Heart crashing into his ribs, Miles pounds on the glass.

There are a few godless seconds when nothing happens, then, one of the people inside moves. The top of the pod slides open. Miles climbs onto the pod and peers inside.

Yes. Three people. Two women and one man and—

"*Mike?*"

The man nearest the window, his eyes flutter open. "M-Miles?"

He doesn't look like Mike. His lips are too dry and cracked. His skin too pale. And yet, he *is* Mike. Just a very ill Mike. A very dehydrated and starved Mike.

The two women do not move.

"Miles..."

He enters the pod and checks the pulse of both women. They're cold to the touch. No pulse. But Mike...

Mike has a pulse. It's weak, but there.

"C'mon," Miles says, hefting his little brother out of the pod. "I'm here now, bro."

All Mike keeps saying over and over is: "Miles."

Luckily, Mike barely weighs one-fifty, making it easy to haul him out of the pod and to the STAV. Only problem is bringing him down into the STAV. The pace is too narrow to carry Mike down.

Miles shouts, "I found him! Need help!"

Shortly, Jenna climbs up the passage. "Are you serious?"

"Yes." He holds Mike so Jenna can see him.

"Oh my god. Okay, hold on."

Jenna positions herself. "Feet first."

Miles stands and gently lowers his brother into Jenna's arms. The woman holds him tight and calls, "Guether!"

No more than two seconds, Guether's deep voice echoes up the passage. "Here. Lower him down."

Miles begins crawling into the hole when a strange sound snags his attention. He's halfway into the passage when a cold, spongy hand claps onto his arm. He snaps his sight up and gapes into quivering, cracked, oozing lips. Blood drips from these lips onto the STAV barely an inch from the lip of the passage. A blistered face twitches. Wide, blue eyes bore into him.

With a grunt, he rips his arm free of the spongy grip. The sunbaked man moans, drops to his knees onto the unforgiving metal of STAV. Blood dribbling down his whiskered chin, the man manages, "P-Pleeeease."

Letting his heart settle a bit, Miles takes a few breaths and shouts down the passage. "We have another survivor."

"I'm here," Guether says. "Send'em down."

Miles crawls out of the holes and says, "We're here to help. Just hold on. I need to help you inside."

"I-It…It…"

Miles nods and goes to help the man to his feet so he can position him better near the hole.

"It *killed* everyone," the man screams.

"I know," Miles says. "Now let's get you out of this sun and get some water in you."

The man coughs. Blood splatters around the hole to the passage.

Grimacing, Miles stoops to help the man up. He grips under both armpits and lifts but the man unexpectedly twists and Miles' right hand slips down the man's arm. And keeps sliding as the man's skin peels away.

Miles gasps, nearly drops the man, then repositions his grip under the arms. "Jesus," he whispers under his breath. Then, "Just hold on, bro. Hold on."

The man moans, blood streaming from the exposed muscles and tendons of his skinless forearm. The skin itself hangs in ragged flaps.

"Help," Miles shouts, heart whip-cracking.

Guether pops his head out of the hole like a damn gopher. He sees what's going on, blinks at the skinned arm and all the blood and—

A large wave crashes into Miles' back. He loses his grip on the man and stumbles forward. Guether catches him before he face plants into metal.

A low growl rumbles, vibrating the STAV.

"Get back inside," Jenna yells from the bottom of the passage. "Get back inside! It's here!"

Miles turns to grab the man and pull him into the passage but he's not on the STAV anymore. He's floundering in the water, trying desperately to swim back to the STAV. Miles goes to help him when Guether latches onto his arm.

Guether shakes his broad head. "No, man. Get inside."

But Miles pulls out of the big man's hand and reels toward the survivor in the water.

"*Miles!*"

He ignores Guether and slides to the edge of the STAV. The man sinks under the surface, splashes up, sinks. Miles, leaning over the edge, extends his arm.

"Take my hand!"

The man gasps, sputters, but doesn't appear to notice Miles there. When one is drowning, coherent thought is nil. Knowing this, Miles scoots farther over the edge, stretching at far as he can.

Water splashes his hand and arm from the man's thrashing, but he's still too far away to grab hold of one of those flailing arms.

He's about to try and stretch more when the water swells. The man rises with the thick swell, still thrashing. Something dark passes swiftly under him. Miles scrambles away from the edge, stomach clenching.

There's no time to do anything.

The swell bursts and a massive maw filled with long, fang-like teeth emerges. Water sprays into Miles. The force is enough to send him scooting across the STAV back to the passage hole. It threatens to drag him back but Guether latches onto his arm.

"Got you." Guether begins hauling him closer to the hole just as the massive maw snaps down over the floundering man.

And it doesn't stop there.

Brief shimmers of bluish scales and each raft is sucked under the water.

Miles freezes, struck by the horror of what's going on. If not for Guether, he might have remained out there watching as each raft is sucked down into the monster's mouth. Before Guether finally drags him into the passage, the thing rises a bit out of the water…and it's massive. A thing that should not be. But is…

The head, as far as he can see, is larger than some houses. The very ocean seems to bend at its will.

Then he's yanked into the passage and the hatch slams shut. Then he's scrambling down the ladder to the floor. Then he almost goes to check on Mike, but Jenna is shouting for him from the cockpit. It's a melee of insanity. He manages a glance into the STAV, sees Emma and the others over Mike, then shuts the cockpit door and stumbles, dripping water, to his seat.

"It's big," Jenna says. "Like, very big. Fast too. Came out of nowhere."

Miles, trying to get his bearings, shakes his head, "Can we get a lock on it?"

"I've been trying," Jenna says, well…shouts, tapping the monitor. "The fucking thing is too fast and we're too close. We need to get out of here."

With Mike safely in the STAV, Miles says, "Gun it. Get us away from here."

"The high thrusters will only last an hour then we'll be dead in the water until the STAV recharges."

"I know the risks. Go!"

The STAV rocks as something strikes it hard. An eerie groaning sound filters through the metal walls.

Jenna taps something on her monitor, then presses the blue button beside it.

Less than a second is all it takes and they're speeding through the water at nearly five hundred knots, shoving him into his seat. All he knows is the dark waters and silvery bubbles like passing stars in warp drive.

It's too much.

A few minutes in and he loses consciousness.

CHAPTER 16

There had been no warning.

One second, they were trying to care for Miles' brother, the next they're all thrown backward as the vessel shoots forward.

Ma tells them all to hold onto something and wait. She says Jenna has hit the high thrusters and they all might be like this for about an hour.

For Emma, who is the only one holding onto Miles' brother so he doesn't get hurt, that hour soon becomes a lifetime.

Geri is still strapped to her seat. Still snoring away as though nothing is happening.

After a while, Jakob helps her place Miles' brother in a seat. It's tough, but they manage and buckle him in. The only thing she worries about is his head. If the vessel stops suddenly, the force might snap the man's neck. So, she struggles into the seat next to him, straps in and holds his head in her hands.

The question that keeps bouncing around in her head is: Why the rush?

What has Jenna and Miles speeding through the ocean so fast? Did they see the creature that destroyed that ship?

She doesn't know. All she knows right now is making sure Miles' brother's neck doesn't snap. What's this man's name? Miles told her a few times but right now it escapes her.

And after a while, she passes out holding the man's head as best she can.

PART 3: JORMUNGANDR

CHAPTER 17

He woke to brisk shakes and Jenna shouting at him.

"Mike is awake. Wake up!"

Miles stiffens in the seat, vision sharpening on Jenna's face. Bright and full of excitement.

"We did it! We found Mike!"

He unbuckles and sits up a bit, letting vertigo come and go before he stands. His back crackles at the movement.

"Holy shit," Jenna says. "You *are* an old man now. I think I heard every vertebrae pop."

"Happens," he grunts and walks toward the door. "Are we clear of that...that thing?"

"Nothing on the scans. I think we lost her, thank the gods."

"Good," he says and opens the door. "Thank you."

Jenna doesn't respond to this last, but he feels her gaze on him. Almost notes the gratitude.

He opens the door and steps into the belly of the STAV.

What he sees stops him a moment.

Mike stands between the rows of seats telling some kind of story. And that's Mike. The storyteller. The guy always had the strange talent to tell a great story, be it fictional or real.

The trouble is trying to figure out if he's being honest or fictionalizing. Or maybe that's just part of the fun.

Even after his ship got torn up and sank by some supposedly mythical creature, after almost all of his crew died, Mike still stands telling stories.

God, Miles missed him.

"So Berky handed me the phone," Mike says. "I said, 'Hello? Yeah, that stripper was my idea', and his wife screams at me something about being disgusting, but ya know...I was so drunk all I could do is laugh." Mike snorts. "Next day, Berky and I woke up in a motel room I don't even remember paying for with eight women and bottles of booze everywhere. Berky, he's on the other bed, two very ugly women snuggling up to him. Naked as sin. Then he peeks over one of these women at me and says, 'Man, I'm never getting drunk with you again. You turn me into a man-whore'."

The only one who laughs is Jakob. A full-on knee-slapper of a laugh.

Miles smiles, shakes his head. "Still telling that same joke. You know, it's been like five years since you debuted it, right?"

Mike turns around, legs a little wobbly, a bright grin plastered all over his goofy face. "Well, big bro...legends never die."

Before he knows it, Miles is hugging his little brother tightly. "I thought you were dead."

Mike pats his back. "Takes more than a pissy sea monster to kill me, man."

Smiling, Miles holds Mike at arms-length, much like their grandpa used to do with them. Funny how those old things sneak their way into one's life as time passes.

"You're a bit wobbly yet," Miles says. "Sit and get some more water in you."

Mike nods, returning the smile. He sits in Sylvi's seat, the smile fading. His gaze finds Miles and when it does, tears glisten in the man's eyes. "I...I tried to save as many as I could, but..." Mike breaks off, bottom lip quivering like it has since he knew how to cry. He slams a fist on the seat next to him. "The fuckin' pods weren't working. Wouldn't deploy. So, I got as many into rafts as possible before she sank on us."

"But," Miles says, frowning, "if the pods wouldn't deploy then how come you were in a pod...with two women?"

"*Two* women?" Jakob shoots Mike a double-thumbs up. "Good work, dude!" When everyone looks at him, he shrugs. "It's how I'd wanna go."

Guether, leaning near the cockpit doorway, arms crossed, shakes his head. "Idiot."

Mike wipes his cheeks free of tears and releases a shaky sigh. "No. The smaller pods were able to deploy, but they hold only three people."

"So...like an asshole, you got in with a couple women and let the others die in the rafts?" Sylvi spits on Mike's boots and glares at Miles. "This has all been a waste of time. Worst mission I've ever been on."

Miles opens his mouth to tell her to calm down when Mike says, "I *was* in a raft. Like everyone who couldn't get into the small pods and make it off the ship before it went down." His gaze drifts away, as if lost in the memory. "You don't know true horror until you've been drifting in the open ocean for three days and your own crew begins picking out the weakest ones on the raft to eat..."

"Shit…" Jakob says.

Mike shakes his head slowly. "The rafts were supplied with two gallons of water. It became more precious than oil to Murdock Jones. Before the last gallon was gone, there was a fight. They—I had to kill one of them. Gabe. Because he slit the throat of another man in the raft for drinking too much water. I can't tell you how much I didn't sleep when the talk of eating each other began whispering around the raft. The last straw was when I dozed off and woke up with Rick, one of the engineers, chewing on Gabe's arm."

"Let me guess," Sylvi said, glowering. "You shot him too."

"No. One of the small pods popped up nearby and I swam to it."

"Why the hell didn't you just dump the bodies overboard, man?" Jakob shifts in his seat. "I mean, that's kinda fucked up."

From the withering look Mike gives Jakob, Miles can tell his little brother is on the verge of violence. "I didn't want to attract anything. Fair enough?"

"Alright," Miles says, feeling the tension building throughout the STAV. "It doesn't matter. Any of it. We have Mike now."

"So…that's it?" Guether asks. "We're not going to search for more survivors?"

"I think that thing ate most, if any out there," Miles says.

"Well," Emma says, "We could at least give it another—"

"Everyone hold on," Jenna shouts.

Miles is just about to reach for something to hold on to when a loud gong noise sounds. The force of something very large throws everyone off their feet except for Mike, Jakob, and Geri. Miles lands hard on both knees. Sylvi stumbles and somersaults over him, somehow landing on her feet like a cat and slipping into the seat between Mike and Jakob.

Somewhere behind him, Emma lets go a squeak.

A loud groaning sound spills through the STAV, then everything falls silent.

Heart crashing, Miles gathers himself to his feet and hurries to the cockpit. "What was that?"

"What do you think?" Jenna points at the monitor. "That fucking serpent is pissed!"

A thick, squiggling line, which takes up most of the monitor, slithers toward them.

"Hit the thrusters," Miles says.

"We're dead for another twenty minutes," Jenna says. "Can't even shoot it."

"Fuck." Miles turns to the cockpit doorway. "Everyone strap in. We're going for a wild ride!"

He slams the door, hops into his seat and buckles in.

"Four hundred meters until impact," Jenna says, voice just above a whisper. "Two hundred meters."

"Will this thing hold up to a monster that can bite holes into battleships?"

Jenna looks at him, eyes wide. "I…I don't know, Miles." She looks at the monitor. "Fifty meters. God, I hope they're buckled in back there. This is going to be bad. I—"

Before she can finish, the world is a spinning, flipping maelstrom. He vomits at some point, not caring where it ends up. Everything is a swirl of dark and light.

Then, gradually, the spinning slows until finally they're still in the water.

Equilibrium trying to take hold, Miles sways in his chair, eyelids fluttering, mouth open. A mixture of saliva and vomit dribble from the corner of his mouth down his chin. For a moment, he doesn't even know who he is.

Eventually, though, everything lurches back together. He sucks in a breath, wiping the drool and vomit mix from his chin and looking at Jenna. Her head is off to the side and she's not moving.

"Je…" He clears his throat. "Jenna?"

She doesn't move.

Miles unbuckles and stumbles to her, almost spilling himself over her until balance digs its heels in. He straightens a bit and pats the side of her face. "Jenna? Hey!"

She still doesn't move, mouth hanging open.

He slaps her, hard, across the face. "*Jenna.*"

She flinches, eyelids fluttering. Her mouth closes, opens, closes. "Whaa…"

He hopes the impact hasn't given her whiplash, or worse. Because he needs her. She's the only one who knows how to control the STAV. He might know a little, but not enough to maneuver in defenses or attacks. Not enough to pilot.

"Captain," he says into her face. "Wake up."

Jenna visibly gags and he backs away quickly. Last thing he wants is to be puked on, then he'll puke again and then it's Pukeapalooza.

But she swallows and keeps it down. Her eyes finally open and she sits up straight, sucking a sharp breath.

"Everyone okay? You okay?" She frowns, rubbing the cheek where he slapped her. "Why does my face hurt?"

"I'm okay," he says. "Need to check on the others. But are you okay?"

Jenna looks around, eyes widening slowly. "I…um…yeah. That was a hell of a hit."

"It was. I'll check on the others."

Knowing she's unhurt, Miles goes to the door and opens it. The moment he steps through, he notices two things.

One: There's a lot of vomit everywhere and, Two: Emma is lying face down on the floor.

Miles goes to her, grabs her up and kneels. He turns her in his arms. "Emma?"

There's a long gash along her forehead and he wonders why she wasn't in her seat when it all finally clicks together. Every seat is taken, if not by a person, then by crates carrying precious cargo. There had been nowhere for Emma to go before impact. Someone had quickly made sure of it too.

In his arms, Miles gives her a gentle shake. There's a moment of fright before she finally groans. A trickle of blood squiggles down the side of her face.

He gives her another gentle shake. "Hey. It's me."

Emma's eyes open, shut, open once more and she's staring at him with those lovely green eyes of hers. She stirs in his arms a bit, looks away and groans. "Wh-What happened?"

"It hit us." Miles glances around and sees Ma sitting up in her seat, blinking. So far, she's the only one who appears at least a little coherent. "Is there a medic kit in this thing?"

Ma frowns, leans forward and rubs her temples with her fingertips. "Yes. Hold on, let everything equalize."

He kind of missed Ma's directness and almost robot-like monotone. Even though, at the same time it kind of drives him nuts. Humans need compassion. Otherwise they're just like any other animal out there. Or robots...

With a sigh, Ma unbuckles. She stands swaying for a couple seconds, then carefully walks toward the rear of the STAV.

Around Miles and Emma, the team comes to and soon the groaning and muttering curses begin.

Mike coughs. "Yeah, that's the bastard that sank my ship alright. Ugh."

"She is very, very angry now," Geri says, sitting ramrod straight in her seat and glowering at everyone. "She will pursue us until she destroys us."

"Why?" Mike spouts. "We didn't do shit to it – her, whatever."

Geri pulls her black, leather back out from under her seat and plops it onto her lap. "That does not matter, foolish boy. She meant to snack on all of you. And one of you escaped. Now she will not stop until this vessel and we are all hers."

"But that doesn't explain shit why it attacked the Cutter in the first place," Mike shouts.

Miles catches a glimpse of Geri's glare, then Ma stoops beside Emma with a green pack.

With a casual glance, Ma says, "She won't need stitches." And to Emma, "Can you sit on your own?"

"I—I think so."

Miles helps her sit and moves away a little. She sways but remains sitting up. The first thing Ma pulls from the pack is a penlight. She tells Emma to look straight ahead and flashes the light over each eye, snapping it away quickly. After a few times, Ma nods. She places the penlight in the pack and brings out a couple of butterfly bandages, gauze, and some tape.

He rubs her back gently, stands, and faces his team. "Look, it doesn't matter why it attacked the Cutter. It did." He points at Geri. "She's the only one with some knowledge of this monster so I suggest you all shut up and listen. She's been right about a lot so far, as well as Emma has been. From now on, I want everyone to listen to everyone and for fuck sake, stop the bickering. You're like a bunch of spoiled kids that didn't get their cookie after supper."

Everyone blinks at him, even Geri.

A silence drifts over the STAV like a fine shroud. Even Ma working on the gash in Emma's forehead is quiet.

Then Geri sighs. "She will not stop, unless we kill her or deflect her until we reach the mainland."

"So," Mike says, "how do we kill her – it, whatever the fuck it is?"

"Fenrir's fang."

Mike blinks. "Ferrari's *what?*"

Miles smacks his brother alongside the head.

Mike scoots over his seat, almost into Jakob's lap. "Hey, *ow.*"

"She said Fenrir. Not Ferrari."

Rubbing the side of his head, frowning, Mike says, "Okay, whatever a Fenrir is."

"See, this is why I was Mom's favorite. I *studied.*"

"Mom told me *I* was her favorite."

"She..." Miles sighs, knowing a trap when he sees one. "You know what, doesn't matter. Fenrir is from Norse mythology, jackass. A demigod, or minor god, whatever. Point is, his fang is the only thing that can kill the serpent and it's attached to a laser burst."

For the longest time, all Mike does is stare at Miles. Then he straightens, a frown deepening on his face. "Serpent?"

"That's what took out the Cutter," Miles says. "It's the, uh, Mid-Gard Serpent."

"Jörmungandr," Geri says.

Miles nods at her. "Yeah, that's her name."

"And..." Mike says. "You believe this, man?"

Miles steps closer to his little brother. "Yes. And if you don't, you're in trouble. I've seen this thing with my own eyes out there. It's huge and we either kill it or let Geri deflect it."

Mike releases a long breath, too long and heavy to be a sigh. "I believe *you*, man. But you gotta admit, this shit is crazy."

"Well," Sylvi says, "what the hell did you think sank your ship? A fuckin' blue whale?"

Mike snorts. "Don't be ridiculous. Those things are extinct."

Sylvi rolls her eyes and walks away toward the rear of the STAV.

Taking the crates out of the empty seats, Miles says, "And whoever did this needs to fess up now. Emma over here got hurt because no one let her into a seat."

Slowly, everyone's gaze drifts to Mike.

Miles blinks. "*You?*"

Mike shrugs. "It was supposed to be a joke."

And here is the Mike Miles remembers the most. The arrogant prankster.

"Are you..." Miles bites off his anger a bit, breathes, and finishes. "Alright, look, I shouldn't have to babysit you or any of the team here. Emma is a part of the team now." He looks at everyone in turn. "And I need you all to accept that fact."

Slowly, Mike begins to smile. "Ohhh, you *like* her!"

"What? No. Yes. I mean, oh for fuck sake. Yes, I like her. But that's not why she's part of the team. She knows the oceans. She knows what to expect in every sector. Temps. Ocean floor. Everything. I want everyone to give her the respect she—"

"Miles," Emma says. "I think they get it."

Ma finishes bandaging her head and Emma manages to stand. "Everyone has been good to me, considering I'm an outsider. Except for the crates in the seat thing, everything is fine."

He wants to tell her differently. That everything is not fine and everyone is giving her an odd sort of hazing. Instead he lowers his head and says, "I'll be in the cockpit if anyone needs me."

He starts in that direction, when Geri says, "If you see her, let me know. I will ready myself for deflection."

Miles smiles, nods, and enters the cockpit. He plops down in his seat.

"Everyone okay back there?" Jenna asks.

"Mike strapped crates into the spare seats so Emma couldn't get secured before that thing hit us."

"*What?*"

"Yup. She hit her head, got a big cut on her forehead."

Jenna frowns. "I knew Mike was an asshole, but I never thought he'd be *that* kind of an asshole."

"Yeah. But anyway," Miles says, wanting to change the subject. "We need to keep an eye out for that Jor – um, the serpent thing so Geri can cast whatever spell she has going on in that black bag of hers to deflect it."

"I see. Well, so far there's been nothing larger than a Great White."

He nods. "Well, if she does show up."

Jenna's eyes widen. "You think it will?"

"Yeah. She's pissed."

"Lovely. And why do you keep calling it a she?"

"That's what Geri calls it. The daughter of Loki."

Jenna shakes her head, staring at the monitor. "Whatever it is, it damaged us with that hit."

Miles frowns, gaze straying to the curved windshield. "Great. Damage report."

"Well, according to the sensors, our right high thruster is crushed. There's a large dent near the side hatch, which might make it difficult to open. And there's the crack…"

He blinks and looks at her. "Crack?"

Jenna points to the far-right side curve of the windshield. He has to squint a bit, but it's there. A tiny, silvery crack snaking from the window molding. Not even an inch long, but a tiny crack can turn into a big one in the open ocean. And—

"We can't deep dive," Jenna says. "Six hundred feet might be our max."

"Yeah," he says.

"And if it hits us that hard again…"

Blowing out a heavy sigh, he nods. "Yeah. How long now before we're able to move?"

"Less than five minutes. I disabled the right high thruster, so we only have the four if we get into trouble again. But I'd, like, not want to use them again." She waves a hand. "Hopefully that old woman really can do what she says she can do."

Five minutes comes and goes and Jenna starts up the STAV. In less than ten minutes, they're speeding through the ocean, aimed back toward the mainland.

The scans reveal nothing following them.

CHAPTER 18

The pain is deeper than the cut in her forehead. A throbbing ache pounding at the walls of her skull. But she doesn't tell Ma this. Although the woman did mention she might have a concussion, which Emma thinks is very likely considering she remembers nothing from the second the monster hit the vessel until Miles woke her up. She doesn't even know what she hit her head on.

Mike has already apologized a dozen times for the prank and she knows he's sincere, but still. It was a dick move and she's not quite totally sure she wants to forgive him yet, even if she says she has to his face. In all reality, she wants to hit him. But hitting him would spark more chaos in the small vessel. And the way things are, she'd probably end up dead.

So, she decides to let her anger go in tiny streams. Purging them slowly.

She takes her seat between Ma and Geri. The old woman has a couple long crystals in her lap. One blue, the other black.

She carefully tucks the bag between her and Emma and gives a wan smile. "I may need you when Jörmungandr attacks again."

Emma frowns. "You think she will?"

"Oh, yes. She is an angry, vengeful bitch."

Unable to stop herself from laughing a little, Emma manages, "Sounds like my sister."

Geri pats Emma's leg. "More than likely a good assumption."

"So, what are the crystals for?"

Geri lowers her eyes, looking at the blue and black sticks in her lap. "They are Venus and Hel. The two tapped together create a song. This song frightens Jörmungandr."

"I know what Venus is, but what's Hel? You mean Hell, as in the Christian religion, or…"

"No. It is Old Norse, though their meanings are about the same. Hel is an underworld where the dead dwell, and it is also a goddess." Geri holds up the black crystal. "This contains the final droplet of her blood."

"Wait," Jakob says, leaning forward a bit. "Gods bleed?"

Geri bursts into cackling laughter and Emma is once more reminded of one of those old witch caricatures. Those old, hunched wretches with the warts on their nose and shrouded in a black, tattered cloak.

Once the cackling eases, Geri breathes, and points a crooked finger at Jakob. "No. A god must fall into our realm in order to bleed." She waggles the black crystal. "These drops were collected during her death. The last living thing from a god or goddess ever known to exist."

When no one says anything for a moment, Geri nods. "It is her that exudes the most power when I bring the crystals together."

"So," Mike says, pointing at the blue crystal (Venus) and grinning. "What's in that one? Dirt?"

Geri lowers the black crystal, cutting a look at Mike Emma can only describe as piercing. "You lack the tact and poise of your brother. Your arrogance is your weakness which will soon unravel your very soul."

Emma's jaw drops just a bit and she turns her sight on Mike. His mouth opens a bit, then clears his throat, rolls his eyes and taps Jakob on the shoulder. "So, how are the Packers doing this season?"

Jakob shakes his head and stands. "Alright, man. What's your deal? Miles always boasted about you. Told us funny and heroic stories of you." Again, Jakob shakes his head. "But what I'm seeing right now...I think that bastard lied to us."

Mike straightens a bit, eyes narrowing. "Do you *want* your ass kicked? Because that's how you get your ass kicked."

There's this second or two of pure pause from Jakob before bursting into wild laughter. The younger man doubles over, bellowing laughter and slapping his knee.

Guether places a hand on Jakob's back and glares at Mike. "Now, see what you did? You turned him into a goddamn lunatic. Again. I just got him back to being only an idiot too, you bastard."

Jakob laughs harder, dropping to his knees on the floor. Howling.

Through all the laughter, Mike says, "I don't see what's so funny."

Sylvi sits beside him, smiles a bit. "Well...let me see. Oh! You're a dumbass."

"What the—"

Guether pats Jakob's back. "You just insulted a former Dagger Point, kid. The Navy's most elite team. And Jakob here, he's sniper, but don't let that get to you as much as he is one of the most highly trained killing machines on the fuckin' planet." Guether clears his throat. "Besides myself, of course."

Sylvi chuckles. "Dream on, mongoloid."

Now it's Guether's turn to laugh. Not the full out gales Jakob is belting out, but close.

"Guys," Emma says. "Let's just calm down. Miles said—"

"And *who* are you again?" Mike spouts.

Emma opens her mouth, but it's Sylvi who speaks. "The one woman you shouldn't fuck with, asshole."

Emma glances at Sylvi and catches a smirk before the other woman turns to Mike again. "Because, Miles said she's part of our team now. But...he never said shit about you being on the team. The one we came all the way out here to save and frankly, I don't think you're worth the risk."

Mike flashes her a sneer. "Fuck off, bitch."

Jakob coughs, straightens, face suddenly drawn. Guether's posture changes from hunched to squared. His large hand lowers to the handle of the knife on his hip. Ma stiffens next to Emma. Sylvi shifts, practically perching on the seat instead of sitting. Her face is something caught between hate and amusement. Not a good combination in Emma's opinion. Especially what she's gathered from Sylvi. And to think, she thought the woman hated *her*.

Still...

"We need to all just calm down," Emma says and Sylvi actually slouches a bit.

Mike stands, eyes darting in their sockets. "I need some fresh air."

"Sit," Ma says. "We're below the surface now."

"How do you know?"

Ma sighs, looks up from her tablet. "The pressure inside the STAV increased. Simple indication we are in a dive."

Mike opens his mouth and shuts it.

Emma stifles a laugh. It's almost comical how they all tore the arrogant man apart. Not funny when Sylvi tried with her, but still...

"Yeah," Jakob says, all sense of humor and laughter gone. His face is cold...eyes stony. "Sit down...Mike."

Mike looks at everyone, a deep frown cutting into his face, and finally sits.

"Atta boy," Guether says.

Jakob sits too, though makes sure there's a seat between Mike and him. Guether plops down between them, grinning.

Geri begins to say something when Miles opens the door and says, "She's coming in hot. Strap in!"

Emma buckles the harness over her, already trembling. Everyone buckles.

Geri pats Emma's knee. "Watch."

The old woman hums and lifts both crystal sticks above her head. Venus and Hel.

Mike snorts and Guether smacks him on the arm. Just enough to make the other man jump. Mike's smile withers on his face.

Geri doesn't stop humming. She rubs the crystal sticks together and sways back and forth in her seat, eyes closed.

Then…she begins tapping the crystals together. They ring, echoing through the STAV.

The tiny hairs on Emma's arms stiffen. The smell of ozone shimmers through the air.

Emma closes her eyes, waiting for another massive hit that might very well be their last.

CHAPTER 19

"This is it," Miles says, sitting in his seat and buckling in. "Can we turn in time to shift off the rigged laser burst?"

Jenna quickly shakes her head. "No. It's almost on us now. No time to maneuver for an attack."

"Then get us out of her path."

"Working on it. Missing a thruster really messes with our capabilities. I just need to move the smallest bit to get out of her path. It'll decrease her impact a little."

"I get that," he says. He points at the crack. "But will that take much impact?"

"No," Jenna says. "I have a trick up my sleeve."

He hopes so but – why does the air feel more electric? Why are all the tiny hairs stiffening on the back of his neck? Why is there a faint whiff of ozone?

Something weird is happening, though he's not exactly sure what.

Shaking it all off, he focuses on the monitor as the sea serpent takes up most of the screen. There's only three hundred meters until impact.

The STAV rises. Now four hundred and forty. Now four-hundred. Before he realizes it, they're at two hundred feet and turning sharply right.

The serpent shoots out below them about fifty meters, swings off in their direction and Miles hopes the scans are in real time and not on a couple seconds delay, otherwise…

But Jenna swerves the STAV to the left and says, "Hold on to your shit."

He's opening his mouth to ask why when all at once it's like his stomach slams into his chest. His feet lift from the floor. All the air seeps from his lungs. And his brain is screaming, WE'RE FALLING, over and over. And I'M GONNA THROW UP AGAIN.

Before his brain can finish any more thoughts, the falling sensation floats to a halt. He gags, head thrumming, and swallows down a hard lump in his throat.

When everything is back to normal inside him, he manages, "Wh – Okay what just happened?"

"Shutdown buoyancy bursts. Reversed thrusters. We dropped from two hundred feet to five like a rock."

Miles swallows again. "Yup. Sure did."

A series of beeps draws both of their attentions to the monitors.

"It's still after us," Jenna mutters and sets the speed to three hundred knots, swerving to the left.

Miles watches, heart stammering, as the monstrous serpent shape on the monitor bolts closer and closer to them. It begins filling up the screen.

"Spin us around," Miles says, eyes narrowing. The familiar chill of battle sheaths his veins.

"What?" Jenna rips her gaze away from the monitor and windshield long enough to shoot him a frown. "Miles, we—"

He curls his hands around his throttle/wheel, fingers finding the triggers with slick ease.

Jenna opens her mouth, closes it, then returns her attention to the controls. She jacks the STAV to the right. The motion is like being on one of those old carnival rides. Tilt-O-Whirl, perhaps. He's pressed into the seat as the STAV spins around and—

"Holy fucknuts," Jenna shouts. "Miles!"

For a breath, Miles freezes, eyes widening.

It emerges through the dark waters, a massive, triangular head dwarfing the STAV. Yellow eyes flash like sunbursts. The head occupies the entire view through the windshield. But then, it does a peculiar thing. The monstrosity stops. A thin curtain of bubbles warble between them and it.

"Miles," Jenna says, pretty much breathless.

"Shh," he manages through the terror gripping him.

Those large, yellow eyes flash again as its head moves left to right, then cocking a bit, as if hearing something only it can hear. To Miles, it doesn't look like a snake, exactly. Similar features, like the triangular head and overall shape, but…it's stouter. Long, bony spikes protrude from the top of its snout. And when its thin lips part in something like a sneer, he blinks at hundreds of long, curved, pointy teeth. No fangs, like a viper, though nothing as subtle as a python. All those teeth, they remind him of a tiger shark.

His finger begins to squeeze the laser burst trigger, as he tilts the throttle and aims for an eye, when the serpent rears. It flashes all those teeth at him, then spans away. Miles' finger relaxes as its body, gleaming green scales, runs by the STAV. It takes almost two minutes before the monster disappears into the dark.

Trembling a bit, Miles lowers his hands from the wheel.

"H-Holy shit," Jenna says. "No one told me how fucking big it is!"

"I did," he says, forcing himself to calm down and think. "I thought you saw that video too. With it swimming? Shit, I didn't think it was *that* big though."

"Big?" Jenna turns to him, eyes huge. "That's not big, that's fucking *huge*, dude."

"Yup."

"But…why did it just leave us alone?"

Miles cocks a thumb over his shoulder. "Geri."

A frown creases her bronzed face. "The old lady? How—"

"Look, I don't know. She has a black bag and says she has ways to deflect the thing."

Jenna doesn't say anything more and turns back to the controls. She turns the STAV back toward land and increases the speed to four hundred knots. They cruise swiftly through two hundred and sixty feet of water.

There's no sign of the serpent now.

Miles stands and says, "I'm going to check on the team. You doing okay?"

Jenna huffs out a stale laugh. "Yeah. Sure." She sighs. "Miles, that thing can swallow us whole."

He kneels beside her. "I know. But we also know Geri's charms or whatever the hell she's got going on, works."

"Are we even sure that's why it left?"

All Miles can do is shrug.

"We need to haul ass to the mainland," Jenna says. "That's all I'm going to focus on right now."

"Good," Miles says. "Maybe she scared it off for good."

"*If* she did, then yeah, I hope so too because that shit is bananas."

He chuckles, squeezes her shoulder and stands. "We'll make it through this. We've made it out of worse."

After a moment, she nods. "Like Romania."

He almost shudders at the thought of Romania. Talk about a shitstorm. A week straight of trying to survive in a forest teeming with beasts. Beasts said to be conjured by an insane vampire in the early sixteenth century. Beast confined to the forest. Ravenous things his team barely escaped from, losing two along the way. If not for the mechs, they would have never made it at all. Those mechanical suits weren't completely safe, but they were better than being exposed to the beasts without. It had been hell, but they made it.

This is bad, but at least they have an entire ocean to maneuver in and ways to stop the monster.

In Romania, they had nothing but the mechs and their wits.

He gives Jenna a hug and she whispers in his ear, "I really missed you." Her warm breath tingles his very soul, yet, he kisses her cheek and hurries out of the cockpit. She's never acted like this before. Usually she's so damned strong willed she rarely shows such emotions. Humorous talk and jokes, but rarely anything as serious as she'd been since his return. He thinks on this briefly, not sure what to make of it, then enters the body of the STAV.

The first thing he notices is Geri holding black and blue crystals crossed over her head and humming some strange tune. Her eyes are shut, but everyone is focused on her. Even Mike.

He clears his throat and they all blink and turn their attention to him. All except for Geri, who still hums and holds the crystals up.

"How's everyone doing back here?"

Emma is the only one who perks up a bit. She tentatively touches the bandages wrapped around her head. "Good. Thirsty, though."

God, why does she always have to be so damn cute?

Miles smiles. "I'll get you some water." He rushes between the rows of seats to the rear of the STAV, finds the steel crate containing the water bottles, opens it using his thumbprint and grabs a bottle.

Before he has a chance to turn around, Jakob spouts, "I'm pretty thirsty too."

He sighs, gets another bottle, and gives Emma and Jakob their water and says, "If anyone else is thirsty, you know where the water is."

"What if our stomach is eating itself?" Guether asks.

"You packed this thing," Miles says. "Go look for food."

Guether puffs out his cheeks. "Well, that's messed up. Give them water but won't get me food?"

"You're a big boy."

Guether lifts a blond eyebrow, "And?"

Miles shakes his head and returns to the cockpit, a little grateful to be away from them again. He doesn't remember them being so…needy. Three years ago, Guether would have already been digging into the food stores. Jakob would already have water. Because, back then, they were self-sufficient killing machines.

Time changes people. Sometimes little by little. Sometimes all at once. Apparently, most of his team changed all at once. Or close to it. Only one consistent is Sylvi, who never even acknowledged his presence besides glancing at him.

"How they doing?" Jenna asks.

"Hungry and thirsty, but okay." He sits. "Anything popping up?"

She shakes her head. "Nothing besides a few smaller blips."

"Good. Let's go home."

"Let's go home…what?"

111

He sighs. "Let's go home, *Captain*."

"Damn right. And we're aimed in the right direction. At this speed, we'll make it in two hours."

A breath, too heavy to be a sigh, issues out of him. "Make it an hour."

"I can't push it too hard if you want to make it without being dead in the water."

"Okay, just get us there."

"I will," she says.

He leans back in the seat, wanting to sleep, though afraid to close his eyes.

CHAPTER 20

A few minutes after Miles shuts the door, Geri lowers the crystals. She shudders. Then slumps forward a bit.

"Don't tell me she just died on us," Jakob says.

"Foolish…boy," Geri says in a low tone.

Jakob makes a show of twitching, eyes all wide. "Zombie!"

Guether lightly punches him. "Idiot."

Emma places a hand on Geri's shoulder. "Do you need anything? Water?"

"Water…"

Emma hurries to get the old woman a bottle of water, bringing it back and twisting the cap off. "Here you go."

Geri straightens, takes the bottle and drinks deeply until the bottle is about half empty. She gasps for breath for a moment, then hands the water over to Emma. "Thank you."

Emma caps the bottle and places it next to her own in her lap.

Out of the blue, Geri asks, "What is your last name, dear?"

It takes Emma a full four or five seconds to realize the old woman is talking to her.

Shaking her head, Emma says, "Oden. Why?"

The old woman turns in her seat, twisting enough to face Emma fully. "You have a variation of a traditional Norse name. I assume you spell it with an 'e' rather than 'i'?"

"Yeah. O-d-e-n. But I'm not Norse as far as I know. Dutch/Irish."

Geri smiles. That same grandmotherly smile that stole Emma's heart in the first place. "Our origins are all mottled, dear girl. Your last name is a key to your ancestors, even if it seems silly."

It takes her a couple of seconds to process this. "You think I'm related to the god Odin?"

The old woman rattles out a chuckle. "No, no, dear girl. But you are of Norse descent, which might serve us later on. Jörmungandr will return, and I might need more strength to push her away next time."

"You think she has some kind of power?" Mike asks out of nowhere.

Geri's eyes close. She draws in a slow breath through her nostrils and blows it out in a whistle. "We all have a bit of power within us. All we need to do is hone it like a fine blade."

"Oh," Mike says.

It seems he's lost his bully attitude. Now he sits, eyes lowered, as though in a deep thought. To Emma, he has this strange sadness about him, like a gray shroud. No doubt he's lost a lot and been through a lot. She wants to talk to him, despite how he's treated her. She wants to help, it's in her nature, after all. To help. Be it other humans or marine life.

She started the charter not exactly for money, but to inform the public of ocean life and how it is today, rather than how it was a decade ago. The oceans have always been dangerous places, but nowadays the dangers are more extreme.

Case in point: The monster serpent thing attacking them now.

Eventually Mike stands and gets a bottle of water from the back. He stands, not looking at anyone and drinks.

"Yes," Geri says, "we all have sparks of power within us." She looks at Emma, blue eyes like marbles of ice. "When the time comes, I will show you what to do."

Emma nods.

"Jörmungandr is frightened now, but she will return with more hatred in her soul. Until then, I must rest."

Again, Emma nods, not really sure what to say.

Geri leans back in her seat and shuts her eyes. Before long, her narrow chest rises and falls steadily and a snore wheezes from her parted lips.

"Damn," Jakob says. "Wish I could pass out fast like that."

"You do, moron," Guether says.

Jakob blinks. "No, I—shut up."

Guether snorts. "Don't get all butthurt."

"I'm not. And didn't I tell you to shut up? Damn giants…"

"You're just jealous," Guether says, grinning.

Jakob straightens, flashes the big man an awed expression and snaps his fingers. "You're right. Those floppy ears *are* pretty impressive. Like a big, pale bunny."

Emma smiles, welcoming the friendly banter between the two men and tries to get comfortable in the seat.

It doesn't take long for sleep to find her.

CHAPTER 21

"We have a problem," Jenna says about an hour after they began speeding toward the mainland.

Miles blinks, shoving his thoughts away for a moment. Mike is the same person, but...a little different now too. He has always been a jackass, but for some reason he's more so now. Actually, he's a bully now as far as Miles can tell. He needs to sit his little brother down and have a real talk. Figure out what's going on.

"What now?" Miles asks.

Jenna stands, wipes a finger along the windshield, just below the small crack, which, he notes has gotten a little longer. She turns and holds up the finger for him to see. It's wet.

"We're no longer airtight in here." She wipes her finger on her pants and sits. "And we can't dive anymore with it leaking like that. Glass will buckle and—"

"I know what will happen," Miles says and sighs. "Do we have any way to patch it up?"

"Ma might have an idea."

He nods and walks to the body of the STAV. Emma and Geri are snoozing away. Jakob and Guether are playing some old card game and bickering over what they might and might not have in their hands. Mike is loitering near the back with the water and food. Sylvi is reading her book and ignoring everyone. Ma...she's tapping away on her tablet like always.

He steps closer to her and she holds up a finger. "One second."

She taps a bit more, then lowers the tablet and gives him her full attention. "What?"

"I need to see you in the cockpit for a minute."

She opens her mouth, probably to ask why, then shuts it again. She nods, unbuckles and follows him to the cockpit.

Once the door is closed, she asks, "What's wrong now?"

Miles slides around Jenna and points at the leaking crack in the upper curve of the windshield. "We're leaking."

Ma's lips press together, forming a thin, pale line on her otherwise brown face. "We can't dive like that and as fast as we're going, the pressure will only make the crack worse."

"So," Miles says. "What do you think we should do?"

Her gaze darts over Jenna's monitor, then fixes on Miles. "If that thing isn't around, we need to surface to make the repair."

"Haven't seen a hint of it in an hour," Jenna says. "I think it's gone."

"Geri says it will come back, but I think I can repair the crack enough for us to at least increase our speed without being breached."

"Well, that answers the question if you can fix it or not, heh," Miles says.

Ma nods. "I can, indeed. It will be a quick patch because I am not aware of where the serpent is or how long before it attacks again, but it'll hold well enough to get us home."

"You could've just said yes," Jenna says, snickering a little.

Ma smiles the tiniest bit. "You know simple answers are against my religion, Amazon Queen." She leaves the cockpit and Jenna bursts out in a heavy fit of laughter.

"She tells jokes now?" Miles asks, between chuckles.

"Yeah, she's gotten weird," Jenna says. "Better check to make sure she hasn't fried a circuit or something."

They both explode with laughter. Probably not really that funny, but stress can do strange things to people, Miles knows.

Jenna brings the STAV to the surface. Through the windshield Miles stares at a blue sky melding into soft reds and pinks. First signs of dusk.

"Alright," he says, "let's get this done."

The body of the STAV is suddenly a swarm of activity the moment he opens the door. Ma is gathering supplies for the repair while the others, besides Emma and Geri, are making sure their AT-40 rifles are loaded and ready. The guns won't stop that monster, but if it helps settle their nerves, then so be it.

"Okay," he says as they gather close. Mike stands a couple of feet away, but he's paying attention. "I want this to be quick. I want lookouts at every point on the STAV. Jenna will be monitoring from the cockpit as well. Geri and Emma, I want you to stay put."

Emma appears on the verge of a kind of rebut, eyes darkening and lips twisting, but Geri places a hand on her arm and all the steam visibly leaks away.

"We will stay close to the cockpit," Geri says. "The crystals may not work this time, but I have one last effort to sway Jörmungandr."

Miles smiles. "In your little black bag, I take it?"

She straightens her posture, mocking a dignified woman. "It is a purse."

He laughs and tells the other to fall out. They move with the same efficiency as they always have. Everyone knows their job, even if he really never assigned anything to anyone, besides Ma and lookouts. One by one, they climb the ladder up the passage to the top of the STAV.

Mike nudges him. "Can I talk to you a sec?"

Miles frowns. "Yeah. Sure. Needs to be quick, though."

Mike leads Miles away from the others as they file out. "Okay, man, listen. I can't go up there. Not with that thing still slithering around."

"It's not even near us anymore. We—"

"I never told you what it was like the days leading up to the final attack." Mike shakes his head and levels his eyes on Miles. "The raft was bad, but those days before, man...I've never seen such insanity spill through every person in such a short period of time. There were murders. People just...killing each other for no reason other than a sacrifice to their god. And get this shit, those same crazies *worshiped* the fuckin' giant snake in the water. It started out slow, whatever the hell went through my shipmates. None of them acted so weird until the thing started bumping us around."

Frown deepening, Miles says, "What are you saying?"

Mike looks away, sighs, then returns his attention to Miles. "I'm saying this thing has strange powers. It turns people against people. We need to be careful."

"Is this why you've been acting like a bigger jackass than usual?"

Mike huffs a breath. "I don't know. Probably. Guess I'm still on guard and don't want to get too close to your team here."

Miles nods. "Fair enough. But Emma is a good woman. A strong woman. What you did…"

"It was wrong. I know. I guess I was just trying to lighten things up a bit and that thing came so fast I didn't have time to take a crate out before she got out of that closet you call a bathroom."

"Make sure you apologize to her, then."

Mike visibly ruffles. "Why? It wasn't that big of a deal."

"Are you fucking brain dead? She got hurt because of your stupid prank. It won't kill you to say you're sorry."

"It might."

"Don't make me shoot you."

Mike chuckles. "Okay, okay. I'll apologize. She won't accept it, but I'll say it."

Miles raises an eyebrow. "And mean it?"

"Yes, for shit shake. And mean it. Calm your tits."

"Good," Miles says. "But I need you up there. You know what to look for in the water."

"I…look, bro, I wouldn't be any use up there."

"You have first hand knowledge of this thing," Miles says. "If it gets by the sensors, your eye will come in handy."

"Dude," Mike says. "What knowledge? Everything was chaos before the ship began sinking. Then it was all about trying to get off the ship. Whatever eye you think I have...man, I don't."

For a brief moment, Miles wants to shake his brother, but, it's only fleeting. He places a hand on Mike's shoulder. "Okay. Stay down here and make sure to watch over Geri and Emma."

Mike nods. "I can definitely do that."

"You better," Miles says, gives his little brother's shoulder a squeeze and hurries to the passage leading to the top of the STAV.

His team is positioned just as he ordered. Every point is covered. Ma is placing a thick film of what looks like plastic over the crack. He watches her use some odd tool, flattening the film over the film. Sounds like a hairdryer and walks over to Sylvi.

"Hey, thanks for not killing Emma."

Sylvi flashes him a grin. "Mission is still young."

He chuckles, gently pats her shoulder and moves on to Guether.

"Anything?"

The big man's gaze never leaves the ocean. "No."

He pats his shoulder and finishes at Jakob.

"Your fly is open."

Jakob rolls his eyes. "I *know*, Jesus, dude stop looking at my package."

A stream of laughter rattles out of Miles. He pats Jakob's shoulder and returns to Ma.

"How much longer?"

Ma glances over her shoulder. "Five minutes."

"Good. Thanks, Ma."

Returning to her work, she nods.

He stands in the center of the STAV, sight drifting from the water to the sky. They haven't been out here ten minutes and already the sky is darkening. Reds and pinks now merging with purples of various shades. It's—

"The fuck is *that*?"

Miles turns in Jakob's direction, noticing the giant V-shape spreading the water coming toward them, and shouts down the passage. "Something is coming! About three hundred feet out."

"It's not our monster," Jenna shouts. "Not even close. Looks like a whale."

Okay, but never in his life has he seen a whale create such a pattern in the water. It's something a shark might make. Something with an angular head.

And it's huge. Three times the size of the STAV and coming in fast. "Everyone inside," Miles says. "Now."

They jerk into action and rush toward the passage. Sylvi is the first one in when the thing slams into the STAV. The force knocks Miles off his feet and he lands flat on his back. All the air gushes out of his lungs in a single whoosh. He rolls onto his side, trying to breath and only managing thin grunts. Someone roars, followed by the wispy chattering of an AT-30 rifle. The relatively new model is supposed to be the best firepower a soldier can carry this day and age.

"Man overboard," Jakob shouts, this is also followed by more chattering of the AT-30.

Catching his breath finally, Miles gains his knees and looks around. Sylvi and Jakob are kneeling at the front of the STAV while Guether blasts away at the water.

Miles stands, readies his AT-30 and jogs to them. Doesn't take him long to realize who fell in.

Ma.

She reaches for Jakob's outstretched hand. Sylvi lays flat, reaching for Ma's other hand when needed. Guether lets loose a thunderous roar, AT-30 cutting grooves through the ocean.

Miles pats his shoulder. "I don't see anything."

Guether pauses the shooting and glances at Miles. "Fucker is down there. Just waiting. It's huge, man. I—"

Echoing up the passage, Jenna's voice. "Get your asses in here! We were tricked!"

Jakob stoops lower, catching Ma's hand and pulling her partially out of the water. Sylvi latches on to her other hand and together they haul Ma out of the water and onto the STAV.

"Get below," Miles says. "We—"

The STAV is slammed again, this time lifting out of the water a bit. Miles stumbles, loses his footing and drops down hard on a knee. Pain slashes up his leg. He winces, but manages to stand and—

"Guether!"

Jakob blasts by Miles, skidding to a stop at the edge of the STAV. Miles limps in his wave, followed by Sylvi.

"What the hell are you doing up there?" Jenna, sounding a little more than freaked out.

Guether swims calmly toward them. As any good Seal knows, panic means you're dead. And right now, the big man is showing the best example of that. Even with a monster lurking below him, he swims with confidence and ease. No floundering or splashing. Jakob, though, is panicking, he leans dangerously over the edge of the STAV. So far, Miles has to drag him back a bit. Miles kneels beside the younger man and reaches out a hand while Sylvi spots them from behind. Ready to pull either back in case shit hits the fan.

Straining, Guether stretches a hand. His fingertips brush Jakob's, then the ocean opens up, sucking the big man down. His wide eyes and gaping mouth are the last thing Miles sees of his old friend before he's gone. There's no sound besides the sounds of frothing water.

Then there's nothing but the gentle sea breeze caressing the failing light.

"G-Get inside," Miles manages, voice thick and full of shock. "Now."

Jakob bats his arm away. "No!" He scrambles once more dangerously close to the edge. Miles grabs him, swings him around and shoves him toward the passage. Sylvi steadies the young man, helping him along as he tries to double back and go after Guether.

"Fuckin' lemme go!" Jakob struggles, but Sylvi has a firm grip and even if Jakob outweighs her by thirty or so pounds, she's overpowering him. Because, Sylvi is a badass like that.

Miles helps get Jakob into the passage and down the ladder. A second later, Jenna shuts and seals the hatch.

"Everyone strap in," Jenna yells. She sounds on the verge of a mental breakdown to Miles.

"You fuckin' jacknuts," Jakob shrieks, bucking and scrambling to get away from Miles and Sylvi. "Lemme go! Lemma go! He's okay. He's fine. We need to go back!" Tears stream down his face. "We need to go back!"

"The hell happened?" Mike asks.

Miles shoves him aside and pulls Jakob close. "He's gone. Let him go. We can't help him. Let him go!"

Jakob's face firms up, reddens a bit, then his gaze lowers and the tears spill down his cheeks. He pushes away from Miles and plops into his seat. "I know."

Miles places a hand on Jakob's shoulder. "We'll get this fucking thing. No more running."

Jakob nods, though doesn't look at Miles.

Behind him, Geri says, "I have one last—"

He spins on her. "No. We kill this thing. I'm done tucking tail and running."

The old woman does not protest. Instead she places her black bag on the floor and smiles. "I was hoping you'd say that."

Miles turns to Emma. She's fidgeting with her hands, but otherwise appears okay. He looks away. "Everyone buckle in. The ride is going to get crazy from here on out."

"Like it hasn't been so far," Mike says, dripping in sarcasm.

He waits for them to buckle in, then storms to the cockpit. He slams the door and says, "Time to kill it."

Jenna half turns in her seat. "Um, okay. What—"

"It ate Guether."

She visibly flinches and watches him sit beside her. "What? No. Not Guether. He…so that's why Jakob is freaking out?"

"Yeah. Last time it hit us, Guether fell overboard. The bastard swallowed him whole."

"I tried yelling at you guys. It tricked the scans somehow. They were only picking up its head until it came into full view. Then I saw it all. I tried…" She shakes her head. "I tried telling you…"

Miles nods and sighs. "I know. I heard. We just weren't fast enough. This isn't your fault."

"Oh, cut the bullshit," she shouts. "I should've known. Now Guether is dead and his blood is on my hands!"

Okay, that's it.

"Stop," he says. "The only one who has his blood on their hands is the monster that killed him." He softens a bit, trying to ignore his pounding heart. On the monitor, the serpent is still there. It's slowly surrounding them with its length like a boa constrictor ready to crush its prey. "We need to go."

She wipes tears from her cheeks, shudders out a sigh, and hits the throttle. Less than a second, they shoot away from the serpent at two-hundred knots. In another couple of seconds, the STAV is jetting at almost three-hundred knots. One moment Jörmungandr occupies the screen, then it doesn't.

"Slow down and spin around," Miles says, hand gripping the throttle, fingers hovering over the triggers. "Time to end this."

Jenna doesn't say anything, slows the STAV and makes a sharp one-eighty turn.

"It'll kill us," Jenna mutters.

"Probably."

He feels the heat of her bewildered stare and grins. "Just focus on dodging its attacks."

But, all at once, the serpent blips off the monitors. Through the windshield there's nothing but darkness.

"The bastard is playing with us," Miles says, eyes darting from monitor to the windshield.

"Did Ma get the crack fixed?" Jenna shifts in her seat.

"I don't know. I'd ask her, but…" He gestures at the watery darkness beyond the windshield.

"Hope she did."

And for a very long five minutes, silence swells the cockpit. Miles absently wipes sweat from his forehead, repositions his grip on the throttle, fingers resting on the laser triggers. He has a plan.

"I'm going to shoot it with the straight lasers," he says, breaking the silence. "When I do, I want you to get me a clear shot to one of its eyes."

"Okay," Jenna says and huffs out a breath. "Is it hot in here to you?"

"Yeah. But not too bad. Focus."

"No," Jenna says and something in her voice makes him glance over. She sways in her seat, eyelids fluttering. "There's…there's something wrong. I feel—" She tumbles out of her seat, striking her head on the sidewall hard enough to create a dull *thunk*.

Now that he's aware, it does feel hot in the cockpit right now. Unusually hot. And there's something else. Something like thin fingers trying to wriggle through his skull into his brain. He shivers, shoots out of the seat, opens the door and spills into the body of the STAV wheezing. His vision blurs and—

He's walking through a cornfield in fall. Their dry, pale leaves crackle and whisper along his clothes. There's a strong musty smell. The purgatory of corn before harvest. He's been through this field a hundred times, he knows, on his way home from school. One of the few remaining giant fields left in the region. Giant, yes, but knows the direction he's going and there's no worry of getting lost in the vast rows of creaking stalks. Iowa. He's in Iowa. Only one of three states still able to grow corn after all of Earth's shifts.

He's deep in this old field when a voice says, "There is no other way."

He stops. He's fifteen and he stops. Where had the voice come from? There is little to be seen through the waving dry, pale leaves. Maybe it's just the breeze through the corn. He continues on, and another few steps, the voice sounds again.

"Worship me, little boy. Worship me and live forever."

Miles, heart hammering, begins running through the corn now. Terror consumes every part of him. Directly behind him something growls. A growl getting closer and closer. The corn crashes and crackles and snaps as whatever is behind him charges.

"Kill for me," the voice says in a growly tone.

Cold claws sink into his back and—

"…real."

Miles blinks, head lolling. His vision clearing until he stares up at Geri's withered face.

"It is not real, your dream," she says. "Jörmungandr is trying to possess you and the others here. Turn you against each other. It is one of her powers I was not sure of until now."

Somewhere close, someone screams. Mike? Jakob? He doesn't know.

"You must not let her inside. Fight her. With all of your will, push her away. Push her—"

The old woman's eyes widen, her mouth opens, bottom lip quivering. A runner of saliva drips from her open mouth on to him. Then she's shoved aside, and Miles blinks up at Mike. His face is a permanent snarl. He lowers a bloody knife toward Miles.

And in Miles' head he hears the voice chanting over and over, "Kill for me, kill for me, kill for me."

He rolls to the side and the knife slices a groove through his arm. Pain sears his flesh and he cries out. Miles crawls away, shaking his head to free him of the thing trying to invade him. It works just enough to pull himself up using a seat.

Behind him, Mike says in a garbled voice, "In the name of our mother, I sacrifice you for long life!"

Miles turns around just in time to slap the knife out his brother's hand and kick the man in the gut. Mike doubles over, gagging. Miles brings a knee up into Mike's face, feeling the nose crunch against his knee. He shoves his brother aside and assesses his team. Jakob is lying in the back, face down and not moving. Sylvi crouches on a seat, one of her knives out, eyes shifting back and forth. Her cold gaze falls on Miles for a moment, then shifts away. Ma kneels over Emma.

Miles hurries over. Ma is stitching up a knife wound in Emma's stomach. God, the poor woman. He never thought she'd have to go through all this. If he had he would have sent her home before they set out.

"She going to be okay?"

Ma nods. "Yes. Not deep enough to puncture anything."

"Okay. Thank you."

Ma nods again, though doesn't say anything.

He finds Geri on the floor. Face down, like Jakob. Blood weeps from the middle of her back.

Kneeling beside her, Miles places a hand on her back. She doesn't move. She's—

Geri sucks in a shuddery breath and says, "U…Use Fenrir's fang. K-Kill her."

And with that, she moves no more.

Miles stands, sight slipping over the remaining team. Mike is curled in a slight U-shape, blood smears his face from the broken nose. Miles sighs, shakes his head and jogs to Jakob. The younger man doesn't move or respond when he shakes him. The reason for this is starkly clear when Miles rolls Jakob over. He's been stabbed six times in the chest and twice in the face. Miles hadn't noticed the pool of blood because most of it was being soaked up by Jakob's clothing.

"No," Miles manages, feeling for a pulse despite already knowing the truth.

Jakob is dead.

He closes the younger man's eyes, cups a cold cheek, sighs, and lies Jakob down. When he stands and turns, he finds Sylvi not on the seat now, but crouching near the wall about five feet from him.

"Sylv?"

She glances at him but doesn't respond. Her eyes just keep shifting back and forth in their sockets.

He'd approach her, but she's one of the deadliest assassins alive. She'd slit his throat before he even managed a word. So, instead, he gives her a wide berth, picks up Mike's knife, and ventures back to the cockpit.

Jenna is still lying against the wall. There's a large, red bump on her forehead.

He crouches, shaking her gently. "Hey, hun. Wake up. You need to wake up."

Jenna groans thickly, head moving slowly back and forth.

"You hit your head," he says.

She gurgles something, but he can't understand it. So, he shakes her again, a little harder.

Jenna's eyelids open, shut, open. Her forehead furrows. Something he's seen even on his own face in the mirror. A sign of a serious headache. A migraine, maybe.

He holds her close, making sure she wakes in comfort. "Wake up, hun. You need to wake up."

And, after a few more seconds, Jenna's eyes open and remain open. "W-What happened?"

"That thing is turning us against each other. That heat and weird feeling was the serpent. It's trying to possess us. It already got to Mike."

She blinks, groans and curls into him. "God, is this even really happening?"

He sighs and strokes her head gently. "Yeah. I'm sorry."

"Sorry for what?"

Miles looks away. "For bringing you all into this."

She turns in his arms so she's looking at him. "Miles, we did all of this for you. We all knew how much you loved Mike." She grunts. "Even if he could be an asshole."

"You feeling okay?" he asks.

"No. Fuckin' head hurts."

He helps her to sit. "I—"

Their world is a slamming, careening kaleidoscope of pain. Miles realizes they are flipping end over end. That's where any real thought ends, though. The pain of being bashed into walls and the seats and the ceiling and floor is enough to strip away any thought.

By the time the tumbling is done, he's not sure what's broken and what's not.

Thankfully, nothing is broken, just battered and bruised. Likewise, Jenna appears only bruised but not seriously hurt.

Miles helps Jenna into her seat and buckles her in.

"It's going to kill us," Jenna says.

"Not if we kill it first." Miles smiles and places a hand on her cheek. "Let's go get this bitch."

Jenna perks up a bit, shakes her head and frowns at the controls. "Yeah we…" she trails off, head bobbing.

"Hey, are you—"

There's no time to react, Jenna brings the knife up and slashes it across his face. Miles stumbles away, back bumping into his seat. Pain like fire spreads over his face and he knows he's been cut badly. How badly, he doesn't know and right now doesn't care.

Jenna unbuckles and stands. She grins, a tiny stream of silvery drool trickling down her chin, knife clutched in her right hand. "You're all going to die."

In a last-ditch effort, Miles shouts, "Let her go, you bitch!"

She chuckles and it's within the dark tones he realizes it's not Jenna any more. It's the serpent making her its puppet.

And so, speaking to the monster, he says, "What do you want?"

Jenna pauses. A frown darkens her face. Then she smirks. "Death. Time has come for the gods to rise up and reclaim this disgusting world."

"We didn't even do anything to you," Miles says.

"You and your small band are examples of my power. Once the world sees, they shall believe once more."

"Are you fucking kidding me? The military will cover our death up. No one will know what happened out here."

Jenna shuffles closer and stops. She points the knife at Miles. "That's why I shall leave you alive to tell the tale. Like my dear son, Leviathan, one shall survive to spread our wrath."

"Lev—You mean you're the mother to the creature that destroyed the old oil rig?"

"Leviathan acted on his own," Jenna says, voice changing into something thicker. Almost gurgling. "Though he knew of my wishes. One was supposed to survive. One to plant that seed of doubt about their beliefs."

Miles draws his pistol and the Jenna/serpent chuckles.

"You will kill your friend that way, but not me. Never me."

"Oh," Miles says, "I will kill you."

"You cannot kill me. I am an immortal god."

"You're not a god," Miles spits and all the seething rage he's been holding back for the good of the team leaks out. "You're nothing but a fucking has been demigod. Forgotten. And that's how you'll stay."

For a second, Jenna's face slackens. Her eyes widen the slightest bit. For a second, the serpent possessing her might actually be worried she picked on the wrong person. But then a long grin, so long Jenna's lips split from the excessive stretching, spreads over her face.

"I suppose I don't have to leave any of you alive. More will come for me and through them I shall plant my seed."

Miles, heart whipping against his ribs, steps closer. "Not if I have anything to do with it, you vile bitch." He lunges forward, slams his pistol alongside Jenna's head.

But Jenna doesn't drop like he hoped. Instead she merely staggers, catches her balance on the seat and bubbles dark laughter at him. Blood trickles down the side of her face, drips from her split lips.

The entire STAV trembles. Form the body of the vessel, someone cries out. Someone else shrieks.

"First, I drive them all mad," a growly voice spews from Jenna's bleeding mouth. "Then I watch them kill each other. Then...I devour."

With a roar, Miles lunges again and brings the pistol down harder.

This time Jenna drops to the floor, not moving. The vile laughter echoes for a few seconds before finally fading and leaving him in cold silence. Blood pools around his boots from Jenna's head wounds.

He blinks, gasps and backs away from the blood. He glances at the pistol in his hand then at Jenna. She doesn't appear to be breathing.

"No," he mutters and falls to his knees beside her, checking for a pulse.

Nothing.

"No." He shakes his head, tears welling in his eyes and streaming down his face.

Up until this moment, he's held it together through sheer will. But now...now...

He turns Jenna over, wincing at all the blood smeared on her face.

"No, no, no." He begins CPR, and despite the blood, tilts her head up, places his mouth over hers and blows. He pumps her chest with compressions, tears dripping onto her. Tears and blood everywhere.

This woman. The one person who always stood by him, even in the thickest shit. The one person who might've even loved him more than his own mother. More than a sister, more than a human, really. Her steadfast love and will to—

The STAV trembles again. This time more violently knocking the balance out of him. He falls onto his ass, gets up and goes back to CPR, even though he knows it's a wasted effort.

I killed her. I hit her too hard. All I wanted to do is knock her out so the serpent would leave her and instead…I killed her. I…killed my best friend.

He's so stuck in panic, he doesn't hear the door open behind him. It's not until a hand grips his shoulder when he realizes he's not alone in the cockpit.

Miles rolls away, grabbing his pistol and bringing it up.

Ma holds up her hands. "Just me."

Breathing in heavy bouts, Miles lowers the pistol.

Ma looks at Jenna, stoops, feels for a pulse and sighs. She carefully inspects Jenna's head, frowns and shoots a bewildered expression at him. "What happened in here?"

"I…I…the creature possessed her." He stands, holstering his pistol and runs shaky hands over his sweaty head.

Ma nods. "I had to shoot Mike."

Miles blinks. "What? Why? Is he—"

"He's alive. Shot him in the leg when he went after Emma and I."

Miles never even heard the shot. Was he really that out of it? Shit…

"I stopped the bleeding. But I tied him to a seat for safety purposes."

His body slumps from exhaustion. The mental kind. The kind that really gets to a person. Ma's clothes are soaked and slathered in blood. Her hands are like crimson claws. Small blood splatters sprinkle her face.

"It's getting into our heads," Ma says. "This isn't just a sea monster, Miles. It's…like a god."

Frowning, Miles' hand drifts back to the butt of his pistol. "You don't believe in gods, Ma."

Seeing where his hand is, Ma also frowns. "No. I don't. But I can't come up with any other explanation right now. I'm sure there is, but I'm not finding it."

That sounds more like Ma, if not a little off. Maybe all the insanity is getting to her. As it's getting to him.

"Yeah," he says, though his hand never leaves the butt of his gun. "Is Emma okay?"

Ma shrugs. "She's been through more than most civilians. But she'll live if we ever get to the mainland."

"Okay. Help me with Jenna, please."

He bends to move his best friend out of the cockpit when Ma says something that stops him cold. "When we get back, we need to tell everyone what happened. We need to plant the seed."

Miles' eyes widen. His stomach drops. A shiver scuttles through him.

There's no time to react. Something hard crashes into the back of his head. He drops on top of Jenna, mind reeling, pain flaring through his skull. But he's still conscious. With a grunt, he rolls off Jenna, pulls his gun free, but the moment he lifts it, Ma kicks it out of his hand. It tumbles across the cockpit in a series of clanks and clutters.

A grin splits Ma's blood-spattered face. The very same lip tearing grin Jenna had.

Rage unlike he's ever felt before consumes him. "You bitch!"

His vision glares red around the fringes, ultra-focused on Ma and the thing possessing her. Like battle fog, all things fall to the wayside and when the red fringe fades, he's on top of Ma choking her.

With a cry of terror, Miles hops off her, body quaking in shudders, heart slamming in his throat.

Ma coughs and rolls onto her side breathing in wheezy gasps.

Temples throbbing, Miles kneels next to her. "Hey. I'm sorry, it was trying to—"

She swings, the back of her hand smacking into the side of his face hard enough to rock his head to the side and a burning sting laces over his skin. She scrambles onto her hands and knees. Her dark hair falls in strings over her face, barely hiding the grin.

"All of those you ever cared about are now gone," Jörmungandr says through Ma's mouth. "You have nothing more to protect or love. Nothing left but to worship me."

"What do you mean they're gone? What did you do?" The one's still alive back there are Emma, Mike and Sylvi. Ma had been too…until now.

The thing toiling inside Ma chortles.

With a cry, Miles latches onto Ma, yanks her to her feet and slams her against the wall next to the open doorway. "What the fuck did you *do*?"

Eyes rolling in their sockets, Ma cackles.

He shifts his weight and slams her into the wall again. Harder. The back of her head cracks against the metal. "*What did you do?*" He slams her again and again, each time the back of her head connecting with the wall and splattering blood. He roars when the light in her eyes dims, then goes out.

By the time he tosses her to the floor like a moldy rag, there's little left of his sanity. Ma doesn't move and now he has two corpses in the cockpit. Both killed by his own hand.

Somewhere, either in his own head or echoing through the STAV, Jörmungandr chuckles darkly.

Chest burning from all the strain and adrenaline, Miles staggers until his back bumps the far wall. Sobs clog his throat. His vision swims in hot tears. A few weak whimpers spill out of him.

It is now he realizes what's going on. Now, as he shivers and sobs against the far wall of the cockpit, he sees it's not his team that's possessed, but *him*. Jörmungandr is in his head. Has been since that weird little dream he had before Geri woke him up. The one with the cold claws sinking in his back.

But the way they looked…the way they acted and those grins…

He shakes his head and tears drip to the floor. He cries out, sliding down the wall, beating a fist against the side of his head. Beating and sobbing and everything is madness. Everything is for her. For her…

Her…

Flashes of memories break free in his mind and float to the surface. Buoys bobbing in dark waters at night. Miles shakes his head again, not wanting to see these buoys for what they really are. And indeed, Jörmungandr tries to coax him away from the buoys by shining a bright light in the distance. A warm, loving light. An inviting light. And he almost goes for it when someone says, "You do it and I'll fuckin' kick you in the lugnuts, bro."

Miles gasps at the voice of his brother. Mike, but he sounds…different. Doesn't sound so full of sarcasm or malice or sadness. He sounds…kind of happy yet disappointed, if that's possible. Or maybe this is all still some fucked up dream? Shit, he doesn't know.

Was any of the mission real?

What is real, anyway? Anything?

Maybe everyone is some AI wandering around controlled by the real humans out there and…

"Oh, for shit sake, dude," Jakob says. "Will you just look at the buoys? I mean, damn."

And no matter how much he looks around, all he sees is the warm light, the buoys and the rolling dark waters. But he doesn't want to look at the buoys for what they might reveal. Be it true or fake, it doesn't matter. What matters is he's not sure if he can see what they offer. He's not sure how his sanity will hold up, as battered as it already is. It—

"My dear," Geri says. "Look at those. Look deep. It is the only way to free yourself from her clutches."

"You got this man," Guether says. "Look at the buoys."

The dead speak, even when the dead should stay silent.

Or are they dead? Maybe they're all still alive and he's in some messed up coma lying on the floor of the STAV and they're almost to the mainland now. Maybe Jörmungandr isn't even real. Because—

"Miles," Mike says. "Thank you for coming for me, but you need to look at the buoys."

Miles blinks and his gaze drifts to the first buoy. A shiny, silver one that bobs and sways with every small swell. He frowns and—

In another life, he stands from his seat and walks into the body of the STAV. When? He doesn't know when this is, but it's fairly recent. Through his eyes, he glances at Jakob and Mike and Sylvi. He shoots his sight to Geri and Emma and Ma. And he's just walking down the aisle between the rows of seats toward the tiny closet that's supposed to be a bathroom. A couple of feet from this, he stops and turns back to his team, minus Guether. Because Guether was swallowed up by Jörmungandr. He's not here. But the others are. His sight lingers on Emma for the longest, then shifts away.

Geri tells him something, but he doesn't understand the words. She has crystals in her hands and a large hammer on the floor. Something that looks like Thor's hammer. Maybe it is. All he knows is he's slightly afraid of it. The crystals hurt his eyes to look at.

His sight lowers to a knife held in his hand. And when he looks, no one but Geri seems to notice. The old woman is saying something. Her words are a muddled mess he can't sift through. Even though part of him tries, *really* tries, to understand. Something else blocks him from comprehending anything except for what needs to be done.

Blink.

His knife blade plunges into Mike's chest. It's yanked out and a fist crashes into his face, breaks the nose. Mike falls to the floor, curling into a U-shape. His vision sweeps to Sylvi, but the woman is too fast. So, here's Jakob. The younger man puts up a struggle and would have stopped the killings if not for slipping in Mike's blood. This minor misstep is Jakob's undoing. Miles stabs him in the chest, stomach and slashes open his throat.

He drags Jakob to the back of the STAV, rushes toward Emma and...

Miles blinks now, focusing on the second buoy. An emerald green one.

Knife high, ready to stab, he comes at Emma. The woman manages to stand and turns just enough, though not enough. He stabs her. A shallow stab, but maybe...

No. Something strikes the back of his head and he loses a space of time. When he wakes, Geri is there trying to tell him it's not real. He brings the knife up and into her stomach. Before she falls, he stabs the blade into her chest and twists, then shoves her aside. It hadn't been Mike at all. Miles was the killer...

He blinks again, gaze falling on the red and yellow buoy.

In this one, he watches through his eyes as he enters the cockpit. Jenna asks him if everything is okay. Instead of really answering, he draws his pistol and beats her over the head until she doesn't move.

In the next breath, he's trying to save her. Maybe Jörmungandr's hold slipped. Then Ma is there trying to help and probably planning on somehow detaining him. Because it's him. He's the one possessed. He's the one being used as a puppet to kill everyone onboard. Because the serpent needs one survivor to tell the tale. To plant the seed.

Jörmungandr changes reality. He saw Jenna with a hideous grin and Ma has the same grin. Thinking Ma is also possessed, he kills her too.

All of this…through his eyes.

All of this…is his own doing while being possessed by Jörmungandr.

It's the final buoy and eventually everything fades to black. The only sound is of his heart thudding heavily in his chest.

"It's up to you now," Mike says before Miles snaps back to reality. "Only you can kill her."

"Fenrir's fang," Geri says. "Right in the eye."

"Use thrusters sparingly," Jenna says.

"The hell you doing, man?" Jakob spouts. "Snap out of it and kill that bastard."

Before he can, the world fills with darkness.

CHAPTER 22

Sylvi cuts the rope binding Emma's hands behind her back and turns her around, hands gripping her shoulders. "He's not him right now."

Emma somehow finds the strength to nod. She doesn't want to look at all the carnage in the vessel right now. And poor Geri…

"We have to take him out," Sylvi whispers.

The stab wound in her stomach burns, but it's a tolerable burn. "You mean kill him?"

Sylvi blinks. "Uh, no. Killer. No, knock him out and tie him up. I can pilot this thing to the mainland if I have to."

Ma has been in the cockpit for a long time. Too long, maybe, Emma notes.

"I know it's not really our Miles. Like Geri said, it possesses people."

"What if he's waiting for us?"

Sylvi shrugs. "Well, it was nice knowing you."

"You think," Emma says, "he'll be okay?"

To this, Sylvi only shakes her head.

After a moment, the woman tells Emma, "Stay behind me." She hands Emma a pistol. "If things go wrong and he gets the best of me, shoot him."

And when Emma blinks at the gun in her hands, Sylvi asks, "Do you know how to use it?"

"I think so…"

"I need you to know so."

Emma sighs, not believing everything that's happened, yet coming to grips with it, inspects the pistol.

"A forty-five," she says and frowns. "Safety is still on."

Sylvi smirks. "So, turn the safety off and let's stop and get us home."

With Sylvi in the lead, they creep toward the closed cockpit door.

CHAPTER 23

He wakes slumped against the wall, staring at the lifeless body of Ma.

But there's one difference he can't deny.

The serpent inside him is gone.

The weight is gone.

The constant gibbering is gone.

He's free.

Miles manages to stand, though his eyes keep flitting from Ma to Jenna and back again.

I did that.

No. It's no good to dwell on that right now. Right now, it's time for…

"Revenge," he says in a growly tone he barely recognizes as his own.

He faces the curved windshield and darkness beyond. He steps over Ma's body to sit in Jenna's seat. The triggers are in the same places on the throttle/wheel as they are on his side. He hasn't piloted the STAV much, but it can't be any worse than a minisub. And didn't Jenna say something about it being like a minisub? He's not exactly sure. Can't remember.

All that matters is—

The door behind him creaks open. He's barely aware of it until an arm snakes under his chin and squeezes, pinning him back into the seat. He gags as the pressure increases.

In his ear, Sylvi says, "Easy, Miles. Easy. This is for your own good."

For his own…

Yes, for being possessed and killing most of his team. Sylvi was spared, somehow staying out of sight when he went on his small spree. She's the only one left, which makes sense because she didn't tell him to look at the buoys. And now she's trying to detain him for his and her safety.

But...

She's going to kill you, a hissing whisper slithers through his mind. *She wants to plant my seed in society. She—*

Miles, growling, shoves the voice of Jörmungandr away. Much easier now that rage and vengeance has replaced her inside. No more are her claws wriggling in his brain. He's free of her. At least for now.

He gasps as Sylvi squeezes harder and red blobs float through his vision, which is melding to gray now. She's applying just enough pressure to put him out, but not kill.

He repeats the latter in his head: Not kill.

There's some comfort in that. After what he did, Sylvi will not kill him. Maybe she knows he was possessed? Or at least believes he might have been?

Even so, he tries to tell her to stop. Tries to tell her they need to kill the monster serpent right now before she does any more damage. Before they all die out here in these dark, cold waters.

He could cut her with his knife to get free. He could do a few different things to break loose of her hold. But he doesn't. Because, maybe it's for the best. Maybe—

"Oh...my god..."

He blinks, gray clouding in. Was that Emma?

The arm pressing against his throat jerks. The pressure lessens little by little.

Miles sucks in a gulp of air, coughs, the gray fog receding. Sylvi's arm slips away. He struggles a moment to sit upright and...

"Shit."

About fifty yards in front of them, picked out by the white glare of the STAV's lights, Jörmungandr stares back at them. Her yellow eyes glow like lamps set in deep stone. Her triangular head is outlined in a dull shimmer. She drifts closer, thin reptilian lips parting just enough to reveal the long, pointy teeth.

Terror bashes through Miles. His heart stutters. All the blood in him turns to ice water. He shifts a bit, not liking how full his bladder feels. For this moment, all he can do is gape at the monster that made him kill a majority of his beloved team. His friends. His family. It made him kill his own brother.

Hate crashes through the terror and rage ignites an inferno within him, thawing his blood. His eyes narrow as battle fog drifts in once more.

"Miles," Sylvi says. "What do we do?"

Upper lip curling in a sneer, he says, "Kill it." His hands grip the throttle. "Buckle in. Now."

Jörmungandr's massive head cocks to the side for a moment, giving Miles a clear shot at one of its glowing, yellow eyes.

Not thinking, Miles squeezes the trigger, only realizing too late he pulled the wrong one. A reddish beam slices through the gloomy water, stabbing into the giant serpent's eye. Its mouth opens wide, it rears and the glowing eye goes out.

"Fuck," he says. "You two buckle in."

From somewhere behind him, Emma shouts, "We have been."

Lips pressing together in a thin line on his face, Miles glances over the controls. He eyes the high thrusters but refrains from using them. No. He doesn't want to run. It's time to do what they should've done in the beginning. Kill the ancient bastard. Instead of trying to run when they found Mike, they should've blasted the fucking thing to pieces.

Jörmungandr thrashes, the force of its movement rocking the STAV.

Before Miles can aim and fire the laser burst containing Fenrir's fang, the sea serpent dives deep into the darkness.

He frowns at the monitor, watching as the thing dives so deep it blips out of range.

And he can't follow. Not with the cracked windshield. Even with it fairly repaired, the patch won't hold in the deep. So, instead, he maneuvers the STAV in four hundred feet of water away from where Jörmungandr dived. He sets in a sluggish zig-zag pattern, keeping a close eye on the monitor.

Minutes pass like hours while he waits for even a glimpse of the giant creature.

It's long enough to wonder if Geri had been all wrong. What if…all they needed to do was shoot the damn thing in the eye? What if…

A shrill scream lashes at his back from the body of the STAV.

Miles jumps, looks around his seat, but from this vantage point he can't see anything.

Another scream blasts through the STAV.

He unbuckles, picks up his pistol and runs to the body of the vessel. What he sees stops him. It leeches away all his strength and he stands there staring at the scene before him, hand holding the gun lowering.

Sylvi slashes her katana through Geri's throat while Emma fumbles with one of the AT-30's. Jakob and Mike shuffle toward her, arms extended, hands grasping.

Sylvi shoves Geri aside and the old woman, blood spilling out her open throat, crawls toward Miles. Her eyes, once a cold blue, are now milky with death. Her mouth yawns open, jaws snapping. Her teeth click sharply.

"Oh, for fuck sake," Sylvi grumbles. She leaps from the seat onto Geri's back. Thick snapping sounds dilute the air as the woman's spine cracks. Then Sylvi drives her blade into the back of Geri's head.

The old woman gurgles something before falling still.

Sylvi yanks the sword out of the skull and spins around just as Emma begins using the AT-30 as a club, obviously not figuring out how to shoot the thing. She beats at Jakob and Mike, but neither back down much. Indeed, they seem to surge forward without pause, back her into the supplies at the rear of the STAV.

Over her shoulder, Sylvi says, "Aim for the heads."

But, as it turns out, she doesn't have to do anything. Sylvi rushes forward, stabs both Jakob and Mike in the head and it's over. Just like that. The men drop like ragdolls.

Sylvi holds Emma for a moment as the woman shudders and sobs, then strides across the STAV to Miles, face drawn.

"The fuck is going on, man?" She gives him a hard shove. He stumbles back into the cockpit doorway.

"It's toying with us." It's all Miles can think of to say at the moment.

"You don't say. I mean, zombies aren't your usual ocean fare these days. I kinda figured that out when you went all fucking nuts on us. How is it doing this?"

Miles shakes his head, gaze falling to the blood twisted corpse of Geri. "I don't know. It's a demigod, according to Geri. I don't think I fully believed her when she said it, but I do now."

"Lovely. We're tangling with a supposed demigod. Because of course we are. Dude, we're fucked."

He looks at Emma, who settles into a seat, head lowered, crying softly into her hands. His sight floats over all the carnage in the STAV. He sees all this and—

A cold hand slap onto his shoulder, gripping so tight the pain is almost crippling.

"Damn it," Sylvi says, yanking Miles out of those cold hands.

He turns and draws his pistol. Ma and Jenna shamble out of the doorway and Sylvi dispatches them with ease. They drop and she kicks them to the side.

Miles glares at the bodies and says, "I'm gonna kill it." Not a she anymore. He can't think of it as anything else but a vile monster. "I *have* to kill it."

"We can't outrun it?" Sylvi sheaths her sword, frowning.

"No. And when the thrusters run out of juice we'll be floating in the water without any way to defend ourselves. We have to kill it."

Sylvi levels a glare on him. "Then let's kill it."

He nods and tells her and Emma to strap in.

"You won't need my help?" Syvli frowns.

"No. I want both of you safe back here. Just in case it gets in my head again."

She doesn't like it, he can tell, but nods anyway. Orders are orders, and even Sylvi, even now, she listens to orders.

Miles hunkers down in front of Emma. When she notices him there she gasps and tries to scramble away.

"Hey," he says. "It's me. Don't—"

"Get away from me!"

Sylvi touches his shoulder. He stands and faces her.

"She's been through a lot of shit during this mission. Let her be for now."

He cocks an eyebrow. "You're friends now?"

Sylvi releases a flat psshh. "You know me. Better not to care than care and lose everything."

Although he knows better, because Sylvi has shown she cares for everyone lately, even Emma, Miles pats her shoulder and tells her to keep Emma safe.

He leaves the body of the STAV, shuts the cockpit door and locks it. He makes sure it's secure. The last thing he wants is to kill anyone else. Jörmungandr is his target.

Unable to shake Emma's reaction toward him, Miles plops in Jenna's seat, buckles in and checks all the gauges and the monitor. Everything is normal. The monitor is utterly blank. Ah, but it's been blank before and they were still attacked. He continues the slow zig-zag maneuver.

And once again, the minutes pass like hours. Slow, mind numbing. If it's the classic way of making an enemy let their guard down by stalling, then he needs to keep alert. Because it's watching carefully. It's waiting. Once it notices a weakness, it'll strike.

There's no warning. No pause. It all happens so fast he can't avoid it.

The monitor is barely through its beep when something slams into the STAV from the bottom. So hard they go from a depth of four hundred to two hundred. The force is like being in an elevator, only heightened ten times with speed. Stomach dropping and face numbing.

And they're still rising.

Still—

The STAV breaches the surface in an explosion of water. He catches a glimpse of the full moon, then the STAV drops below the surface. He blinks at the dark waters, then growls deep in his throat.

"You fucking pussy," he shouts. "You can't kill *me*!"

But there's nothing on the monitor now.

He dives to around three hundred feet, glaring at everything and anything as rage boils and froths.

"Where the hell are you?" he whispers, propelling the STAV toward mainland again.

Still, there's nothing.

He does not zig-zag this time. This time he figures out to remain sentient and have the STAV turn in every direction in slow intervals. Probably not the safest maneuver, but it's all he can think of to do.

"Come on, you bastard," he says to the empty cockpit. "Come on."

Then, the faintest beep from the monitor sounds. Jörmungandr slithers over one hundred feet above. Miles stops the STAV facing toward the surface and nudges the thrusters a bit. The monitor picks it up. Not in full, but at least the end he's looking for. The head.

It passes by without an attack. Passes without pause.

"Oh no you don't," Miles says, voice barely a voice at all. More like a growl.

He hits the mid-thrusters, jolting the STAV into four hundred knots within six seconds. He shuts the mid-thrusters off for fear of draining too much power. If high-thrusters drain it all, mid-thrusters are a slow death. Or so he thinks. Truth be told, he just doesn't know.

Despite everything, though, he drifts within thirty feet of the nightmarish serpent. A creature that can not only devour but invade the minds of the living…and the dead.

His gaze narrows on the shimmering outline of the monster and shoots a laser at it.

Jörmungandr swerves away, then doubles back. He still can't fully judge its length.

Before he knows it, the serpent is glaring at him through the windshield.

In the cockpit (or is it all in his head?) Jörmungandr whispers, "Your weapons of man cannot harm me. Kill the women and spread my seed to society. This is your final chance to do what's right."

His heart doesn't pound, nor his blood run cold. No. All is vengeance now. All is hate. All is…red.

The serpent slithers closer, shifting just enough. Yes…just enough.

His finger caresses the laser burst trigger as he aims for the glowing, yellow eye. "Fuck you."

Jörmungandr visibly stiffens, as though in shock.

Miles squeezes the laser burst trigger, a shout of triumph exploding out him.

Until he realizes the burst doesn't contain the fang.

It strikes the serpent hard, though, extinguishing the yellow eye. A black swirling of what he assumes is blood fills the water.

In a moment, the STAV quakes. A series of violent groans and creaks sounds.

"Foolish," Jörmungandr says. "I was about to let you live. But now…"

The STAV groans some more. Something hisses and a pressure alarm blares.

The patched crack sneaks free of the patch and grows, spiderwebbing the corner.

"I'll crush this vessel and you will drown," the serpent says. "Unless you kill those two women right now." The STAV shakes violently. "Think about it, Miles. You can live through this. You can come out a hero, just like that piece of shit that killed my beloved Leviathan. You can go on and make a better life for yourself." And before his mind's eye he sees just how beautiful life will be if he chooses to do as the serpent says. He sees a life full of love and warmth. Of a wife and child. He sees a nice two-story house in the woods with a lake nearby and oh, there's a dog and the windshield cracks some more and water leaks through and—

"*No*," he roars, aims at the nearest eye, and pulls the trigger.

He catches only a slight peek of the fang attached to the laser burst cap before it plunges into the luminous eye.

Either in his head or everywhere, Jörmungandr shrieks. A high-pitched sound. He clasps his hands over his ears, but that doesn't help much.

The massive serpent thrashes. Realizing how insane the thrashing is, he hits reverse. Not soon enough.

Jörmungandr's head crashes into the STAV, knocking the vessel aside. It's a tumbling, flipping world before the emergency thrusts stabilize the STAV.

If Miles had anything left in his stomach he'd be vomiting. As it is, he's stuck in a slightly nauseated state. Once this passes he checks the monitor.

The serpent is still there. Still very close but…

The STAV floats toward the surface. Even as he uses the mid-thrusters to dive, the vessel is being pulled upward.

He cuts the thrusters and allows the STAV to float. Because wasting juice trying is stupidity.

The STAV emerges out of the ocean, bobbing on the surface during what appears to be a mild storm.

And still Jörmungandr remains on the monitor.

Miles slumps, suddenly struck with weariness. Be it from everything that has happened or lack of sleep, or both. He slumps.

But he can't pass out now. The monster might not be dead. And he needs to check on Emma and Sylvi. He needs to…

CHAPTER 24

Warmth spreads over him and his eyes flutter open. He squints at the sunlight glaring at him through the windshield.

A groan finds its way out of his throat and he tries curling in the seat to avoid the sun.

It's no use.

He licks his lips though it does little to wet them. When was the last time he'd drunk anything? Not sure. A few hours? A day? Doesn't matter, he's damn thirsty right now.

Miles unbuckles, sits up. His back is a series of crackles and pops. He waits for his body to come to terms with waking, then stands and unlocks the cockpit door.

Neither Emma nor Sylvi are in the body. Unless they're both in the tiny bathroom, but he can't see this as a possibility. Instead of searching for them, he steps through the gore of his dead teammates to the water. He screws off a cap from a bottle and drinks deeply until the bottle is gone. He grabs another bottle, opens it, but this time drinks casually as he sighs and checks the bathroom just in case. The women aren't there.

After a moment, he stops at the passage leading to the top of the STAV. The hatch is open. How it was opened without him doing so from the cockpit, he doesn't know.

But...he found the two women. Or at least, he hopes so and not that Jörmungandr coaxed them out to their deaths.

Even so, he grabs two more water bottles and climbs the ladder to the opening.

"It's about damn time," Sylvi says the moment he climbs out of the passage. "Come enjoy the view."

Miles squints from the glaring sun but finds Emma and Sylvi sitting on the edge of the STAV, legs dangling over the edge.

"Get away from there," he says. "It..."

He skids to a stop and turns in a slow circle. As his sight adjusts, the reality of what he's seeing comes into full focus. For the longest time, he cannot speak. He can't move other than turning.

Partially floating belly-up on the lazy waves of the Pacific, is the serpent. Its stark white belly scales glint in the sun. The majority of the thing appears to snake out and away for miles, but the head is near. It thunks into the STAV from time to time from larger waves.

The head is twice as large as the STAV, but when the waves loll it to the side he spots Fenrir's fang still stuck in its eye.

"Holy shit," he manages.

"Yeah. It's one dead motherfucker," Sylvi says.

Breaking free of his shock, Miles walks over to the women and hands them the water bottles. Emma gives him a cautious look, but eventually smiles and says thanks. There will be no convincing her he's okay now. She witnessed him brutally kill people. One of them his own brother. A fact that hasn't really struck home to him yet, but he imagines will sooner or later. And when it does…what's to stop him from pulling the trigger on himself.

But for now, he sits beside Emma, legs dangling over the edge and takes a drink of water.

All three of them stare at the sun kissed blue/green water and the floating corpse of an Old Norse demigod.

A shrill cry sounds from above and a seagull lands on the white belly of the serpent. It pecks at the scales.

Miles takes a long pull from his bottle of water, sighs, shakes his head, and says, "Fucking annoying little bastard."

He ignores the eyes on him and drinks some more water.

His gaze drifts to the rolling waters lapping at the side of the STAV.

What other monsters lurk below?

What waits in the fathoms?

What stalks these dark waters?

The world has changed, and anything is possible.

He's just glad this shit over.

THE END

**SEVERED**PRESS

CHECK OUT OTHER GREAT DEEP SEA THRILLERS

THEY RISE
by Hunter Shea

Some call them ghost sharks, the oldest and strangest looking creatures in the sea.

Marine biologist Brad Whitley has studied chimaera fish all his life. He thought he knew everything about them. He was wrong. Warming ocean temperatures free legions of prehistoric chimaera fish from their methane ice suspended animation. Now, in a corner of the Bermuda Triangle, the ocean waters run red. The 400 million year old massive killing machines know no mercy, destroying everything in their path. It will take Whitley, his climatologist ex-wife and the entire US Navy to stop them in the bloodiest battle ever seen on the high seas.

SERPENTINE
by Barry Napier

Clarkton Lake is a picturesque vacation spot located in rural Virginia, great for fishing, skiing, and wasting summer days away.

But this summer, something is different. When butchered bodies are discovered in the water and along the muddy banks of Clarkton Lake, what starts out as a typical summer on the lake quickly turns into a nightmare.

This summer, something new lives in the lake...something that was born in the darkest depths of the ocean and accidentally brought to these typically peaceful waters.

It's getting bigger, it's getting smarter...and it's always hungry.

CHECK OUT OTHER GREAT
DEEP SEA THRILLERS

SEA RAPTOR
by John J. Rust

From terrorist hunter to monster hunter! Jack Rastun was a decorated U.S. Army Ranger, until an unfortunate incident forced him out of the service. He is soon hired by the Foundation for Undocumented Biological Investigation and given a new mission, to search for cryptids, creatures whose existence has not been proven by mainstream science. Teaming up with the daring and beautiful wildlife photographer Karen Thatcher, they must stop a sea monster's deadly rampage along the Jersey Shore. But that's not the only danger Rastun faces. A group of murderous animal smugglers also want the creature. Rastun must utilize every skill learned from years of fighting, otherwise, his first mission for the FUBI might very well be his last.

OCEAN'S HAMMER
by D.J. Goodman

Something strange is happening in the Sea of Cortez. Whales are beaching for no apparent reason and the local hammerhead shark population, previously believed to be fished to extinction, has suddenly reappeared. Marine biologists Maria Quintero and Kevin Hoyt have come to investigate with a television producer in tow, hoping to get footage that will land them a reality TV show. The plan is to have a stand-off against a notorious illegal shark-fishing captain and then go home.

Things are not going according to plan.

There is something new in the waters of the Sea of Cortez. Something smart. Something huge. Something that has its own plans for Quintero and Hoyt.

CHECK OUT OTHER GREAT DEEP SEA THRILLERS

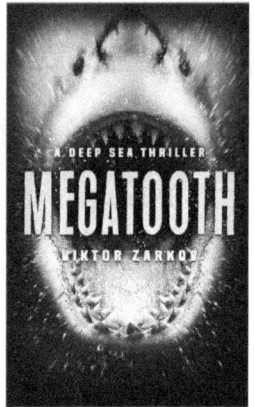

MEGATOOTH
by Viktor Zarkov

When the death rate of sperm whales rises dramatically, a well-respected environmental activist puts together a ragtag team to hit the high seas to investigate the matter. They suspect that the deaths are due to poachers and they are all driven by a need for justice.

Elsewhere, an experimental government vessel is enhancing deep sea mining equipment. They see one of these dead whales up close and personal...and are fairly certain that it wasn't poachers that killed it.

Both of these teams are about to discover that poachers are the least of their worries. There is something hunting the whales...

Something big
Something prehistoric.
Something terrifying.
MEGATOOTH!

BLOOD CRUISE
by Jake Bible

Ben Clow's plans are set. Drop off kids, pick up girlfriend, head to the marina, and hop on best friend's cruiser for a weekend of fun at sea. But Ben's happy plans are about to be changed by a tentacled horror that lurks beneath the waves.

International crime lords! Deep cover black ops agents! A ravenous, bloodsucking monster! A storm of evil and danger conspire to turn Ben Clow's vacation from a fun ocean getaway into a nightmare of a Blood Cruise!